'Don't...stop.'

Mary Ellen's breathles[...]
Greg's husky laughter[...]
then began to tease her other nipple, nudging,
tasting, taunting. When his hand trailed lower,
she hesitated. 'Don't let me, Mary,' he repeated,
his voice low and throaty.

With a slow, soft touch, he stopped her breath.
The feeling was delicious, wondrous... Her eyes
drifted closed, her body swayed to some
tantalizing inner music.

'Look at me, Mary Ellen.' Greg's voice intruded
into her inner fantasy.

She looked down. His mouth was barely inches
away from her breast. His hazel eyes stared up at
her, implacable as cold steel, except for the inner
light behind them that proclaimed the heat he
was feeling was as overwhelming as hers. 'Know
who I am. Know that it's me with you,' he said,
and it was more a command than a request.

Her voice shook as she spoke. 'I know you,
Greg. I'd know you anywhere.'

He smiled. 'Then know this, too, our love was
meant to be...'

Rita Clay Estrada is one of Temptation's® best-loved authors. Not only has she written more than twenty books for her fans, she is also co-founder and first president of the Romance Writers of America. And yet, she didn't intend to be a writer. She studied art and psychology, worked as a model, a secretary, a salesperson, a bookstore manager…and the list goes on to this day.

Rita is also a mother, and a woman whose family is very important to her. *Dreams* was dedicated to and inspired by Rita's aunt Mary Ellen Gallagher, whom she describes as independent, feisty and interesting (much like Rita herself). Rita's next Temptation novel, coming later in the year, will feature yet another Gallagher woman and the man who captures her heart.

Other novels by Rita Clay Estrada

Temptation®
THE STORMCHASER
LOVE ME, LOVE MY BED
WISHES

DREAMS

by

Rita Clay Estrada

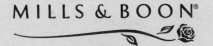

MILLS & BOON®

For the second Gallagher sister, Mary Ellen Straub—
you're a winner, Aunt.

*MILLS & BOON and MILLS & BOON with the Rose Device
are registered trademarks of the publisher.
TEMPTATION is a registered trademark of
Harlequin Enterprises Limited, used under licence.*

*First published in Great Britain 1999
by Harlequin Mills & Boon Limited,
Eton House, 18-24 Paradise Road, Richmond, Surrey TW9 1SR*

© Rita Clay Estrada 1998

ISBN 0 263 81653 2

21-9903

*Printed and bound in Great Britain
by Caledonian International Book Manufacturing Ltd, Glasgow*

1

LIKE SOME OF THE MEN Mary Ellen Gallagher had met in the past, old-fashioned screws were harder and tougher than today's wimpy variety. She dug at a particularly stubborn screw imbedded in the solid oak cabinet, cursing quietly under her breath as she did so. Older screws had resilience, a steel backbone. And damn it, this old house-cum-office she'd chosen to buy and renovate had a lot of stubborn, old-fashioned screws.

"What in heaven's name are you doing?" Edie, her secretary, stood at the kitchen door, hands on her hips, staring in disbelief.

Mary Ellen kept her concentration on the recalcitrant screw. "I forgot to charge the electric drill last night. I've got to take off the rest of these cabinet doors by hand if I'm going to get anywhere this morning."

"I'm impressed." The deep whiskey-rich voice that replied certainly didn't belong to Edie. "Most women would call in a repairman."

Brushing midnight black hair away from her eyes, Mary whirled around, and her brown-eyed gaze was caught immediately by a pair of pale hazel eyes belonging to a very imposing man. He was dressed in an expensive-looking, steel gray suit that highlighted those pale eyes, and he wore a warm, sexy smile that curved his full lips and sent dimples slashing all the way down his cheeks to his strong jawline. His potent appeal was magnetic.

Thank goodness, Edie brought her back to reality. "Greg Torrance, this is Mary Ellen Gallagher. Mary, Mr. Torrance wanted to see some of your work, so I showed him the video you filmed last month of the office supply house. Still, I thought it might be better if you spoke to him."

Mary wished Edie had left her potential client in the newly completed waiting room at the front of the old house. Though the walls were freshly painted and might still be a little tacky, and the new grout between the floor tiles might not have hardened completely, it was a much better site for business than this half-demolished room.

Following his light-eyed gaze, she glanced down and realized the situation was even worse. Although it was February, she was doing "grunt" work, so she was wearing a pair of shorts and a T-strap jogging bra with a see-through webbed shirt over it. Not the power suit she usually wore when she wanted to impress someone with her professionalism.

On the other hand, the kitchen was toasty warm, thanks to the oven. Earlier, she'd put in some refrigerated cinnamon rolls, which were now filling the kitchen with a wonderful yeasty aroma.

Greg Torrance must have smelled them, too. "An entrepreneur, repairman and cook, all rolled into one woman. That's a powerful package," he murmured.

"Why?" she asked.

"Because most men can only do one thing really well, and that's usually business oriented. The rest, they get others to do."

"And what is it that *you* do really well, Mr. Torrance?" she queried, giving him a haughty look, even though she knew that intimidation wasn't likely to work, not in this messed-up room, and dressed as she was.

His smile was just as devastating the second time around. "I said 'most men,' Ms. Gallagher. I didn't say me."

"I stand corrected." She forced herself not to smile in return. "And what are your specialties?"

"Well, the one that's up for discussion is magnetic pumps. I'm looking for someone who can produce a sales info commercial for our company that makes magnetic pumps look intriguing, exciting and fun."

"Interesting. And just what *is* a magnetic pump?"

He gave a husky laugh. "That would take a long explanation."

"Try me," she said.

He shrugged. "Okay. Magnetic pumps are used to drive caustic chemicals through pipelines. Since fluids don't go through the engine itself, if the motor breaks down, workers can repair or replace it without exposing themselves to the chemicals. Plus, it also helps an engine last longer because acids aren't touching any moving parts. Corrosive fluids are pushed through pipes by a series of magnetic sections that pump them through flow tubes."

Mary Ellen stepped off the countertop to the stepladder, then climbed down to the floor. Facing him with as much dignity as she could muster, she said, "You don't hesitate to offer a tough job, do you?"

He shrugged broad shoulders. "I know it's not a picnic. That's why I figured an independent filmmaker would be best for my needs."

"But I specialize in VHS film. Why would you choose this medium, when most companies prefer to go for what's considered to be professional sixteen millimeter? That's what the big public relations firms use."

"Public relations firms know even less about pumps than you do. Besides, this film will be seen on TVs in boardrooms and at trade shows, so I think it should be filmed for VCR. A film shown in that medium should be shot in that medium."

Mary Ellen cocked a brow knowingly. "To say nothing of its being cheaper."

He didn't even flinch, responding with an easy nod of agreement.

Edie, whose gaze had been darting back and forth between them as if she was watching a tennis match, murmured, "I'll be in the reception area.'' She disappeared quickly, a smile on her face.

''Please check on the Mervyn account, will you?'' Mary Ellen called. ''We've got to start filming next week.''

''Will do,'' Edie caroled from the other room.

Both knew it wasn't the major department store chain, but a jewelry wholesaler who wanted a video of her line to show at parties. But it was always better to let a client know there was competition for her time, Mary Ellen believed. Feeling more confident, she filled the teapot with water and placed it in the microwave, which was plugged in, to an extension cord that hung from the ceiling, where the only light in the entire kitchen glowed dimly. It reminded her of how much more money she needed to renovate this place.

''Tea?'' She was sure he would turn it down.

''I'd love some.''

Reaching inside the cabinet, she found two cups and a couple of packages of tea.

''Funny you should mention Iris Mervyn's name. She's one of the people who recommended you to my partner.''

''Oh?'' So much for pretending she had a huge account and didn't need to impress this potential new customer. ''Do you know her?''

Greg Torrance strolled to the kitchen table and pulled out a chair. ''May I?'' he asked.

She nodded.

''She's a social acquaintance.'' He sat down,

his hazel eyes watching her every move as she prepared the tea. "We occasionally meet at parties."

Mary Ellen pulled steaming cinnamon rolls from the oven and set the flat tin on the stove burners. Then, with a spatula, she placed the piping hot buns on a plate. Sitting across from him, she prayed her stomach wouldn't growl before she soothed her hunger.

"Dig in," she ordered, picking up a bun and warning herself not to stuff the whole thing in her mouth. Nevertheless, she polished it off in less than a minute.

"Tell me about your business," he said, as he added sugar to his tea and stirred.

"Edie has a brochure in the front."

"I don't want a brochure. I want you to tell me," he demanded.

"Edie also has a list of clients who will be happy to testify on how my film-making abilities have improved their business."

"I'll read it later."

Mary took a sip of tea while she gathered her thoughts. "I started in this business when I was fifteen, taking photographs for the high-school paper. By the time I was seventeen, I was good enough to work for a professional studio that supplied photographers for weddings, parties and such."

"Enterprising."

"Wasn't it though?" She needed this job and the money it would bring her, and wasn't foolhardy enough to pretend otherwise, so she continued with her life story. "By the time I was twenty, I'd won two awards from the state filming commission. Since then, I've gathered a very long list of credentials."

One wicked brow lifted. "In all those years since then?" he asked dryly.

Obviously, he thought she didn't look old enough to be so experienced, but that didn't mean she was a fake. "Steven Spielberg was one of the youngest directors in his peer group, too, Mr. Torrance. I won't apologize for my age."

"Which is?"

Adrenaline rushed through her body, but ironically, the more excited she became, the calmer she acted. There was nothing like a challenge. "How old are *you*?"

He brushed her question aside. "My age isn't relevant. I'm not being hired."

"No, but I'm not sure I can work for a man who might be too young to run a major company or too old to appreciate innovation."

Appreciation of her quick comeback was reflected in his gaze. "I'm thirty-three."

"I'm twenty-nine."

"And innovative."

"…And talented." She finally allowed herself a satisfied grin. "One of the best."

"How long would it take you to complete a project like this?"

"We can discuss that when you and I sit down to do business."

By the surprised expression on his face, she suspected he wasn't used to being put off. "What are we doing now?"

"Sharing a cup of tea." She nodded at the plate of cinnamon rolls and he took one. "And getting to know each other."

"That's important?" he asked, before taking a big bite of his roll.

"Certainly." She eyed him with far more assurance than she felt. "If you don't know me, you can't trust me. If you can't trust me, you won't let me do my job without interference. If I can't do my job, I won't give you the finished product we both deserve. If I don't do that, then neither one of us will be happy."

His rich, deep laugh washed over Mary like warm, thick honey. For a long, easy moment she basked in the heat, and, the sight of him. He was handsome when he was somber and quiet; he was absolutely devastating when he laughed.

She watched him lick the sugary frosting from his thumb—all that remained of the cinnamon bun—and experienced an empty feeling in the pit of her stomach.

"You have a remarkable way of looking at things, Ms. Gallagher, and I'm very impressed. Do you suppose now we could take this conversation to the next level and talk about doing business together?"

Mary Ellen's urge to eat one more roll was suddenly gone and forgotten. "I'd be happy to," she said. Right now, she was happy that she remembered her name. Never had she been so irresistibly drawn to a person. A project, maybe, but never a person. Quickly, she stood and extended her hand. "It's been pleasant meeting you, Mr. Torrance. Is there anyone else who would be working with you on this project? You mentioned a partner...."

"Yes," he replied, and the smile she was getting addicted to so quickly disappeared. "I have a partner who will probably want to put in her two cents worth. Which, believe me, isn't a bad thing. Her incisive input is worth its weight in gold."

"Fine. Will you bring her with you the next time?"

He stood and, at last, took her outstretched hand. Mary Ellen was finding it almost impossible to maintain the businesslike attitude she'd kept up so far, despite being in the middle of a demolished kitchen, wearing shorts and a skimpy top. But she gave it her best try. And then their hands came together. At first touch, she felt the heat of his body down to her very core. He held on to her hand, across the table, and looked into her eyes. "Next time," he said. "Let's meet on my turf."

Mary cleared her throat. "Good idea." She swallowed hard. "I can get a better sense of the business. Why don't you set up an appointment with my secretary for next week?"

His grin peeped out as he let go of her hand

and placed his fists on his hips. "Why don't I just do that?"

"In that case, Mr. Torrance," she said, struggling for the right tone—casual yet businesslike, "I'll see you soon."

He didn't move. He remained standing by the table with his hands on his hips, looking around the kitchen. He shook his head, and she knew that he knew what kind of work was in store for her. Mary could easily visualize what he was seeing—the place as a hopeless mess....

"I envy you your work," he said, surprising her. "It's fun to see what develops as you go."

"I thought you said you hired people for this kind of manual labor?"

He raised his brows. "I said 'most' men did. Don't judge by the clothing, Ms. Gallagher, and I won't do the same to you. And just for the record, I love doing renovations. You can lose yourself in the work, and when you're finished, it's as if you've been on vacation and actually accomplished something at the same time."

"Some people get that feeling even when they're working in a suit," she countered, just for the sake of argument.

"And some people get it both ways." He swept his gaze over everything—from the old wooden floor to the rotted windowsills. "It'll be a challenge. But a satisfying one."

"I think so, too."

She noticed that a certain stiffness had crept into his demeanor, as if he was distancing himself emotionally from her. "Good luck, Ms. Gallagher."

"Thank you," she replied and strangely enough, felt a twinge of emptiness as he left the room and headed down the hall.

Standing by the table and staring at the seat he had occupied, she waited for the sound of the front door shutting. When the latch finally clicked, she realized her heart was beating wildly and her thoughts were flying. She put it down to the possibility of a good-paying job doing something innovative and original, doing her favorite thing. And then her thoughts skipped back to Greg Torrance. She wondered if he was single, and if he was, if he ever dated business associates....

Wrong thought! She was daydreaming, which was against the new rules. No more dreaming, day or night, she'd vowed. It hurt too much when reality hit afterward.

Besides, wondering about the handsome Mr. Torrance was totally off topic. This was a plum job they were negotiating, not a date, and she already had more to do than a one-armed paperhanger. She didn't have time for a social life.

WHEN IRIS MERVYN PHONED and asked her to drop over, Mary Ellen accepted with a little surge of excitement zinging through her veins. Iris would be able to answer her questions about Greg Torrance.

All week long, ever since he'd come to her

house, curiosity had been killing her. She dreamed about the man, mused about him over morning coffee. By bedtime, she'd have thought of him at least ten times throughout the day.

She found herself wondering what it would be like to move in his elevated social circle, to see what he saw, to spend what he probably spent in a evening, surrounded by Houston's elite. At the same time, she reminded herself to get a grip—his company made magnetic pumps, for heaven's sake! That wasn't so elite—that was dirty, sweaty work. And she'd imagined him dirty and sweaty....

She leaned on the doorbell of the Mervyns' River Oaks town home. The door flew open instantaneously.

"So glad you're on time," Iris said, her smile as big as the room behind her. She ushered Mary into the brick-floored entry. "I've been bored to tears with no one to talk to this morning. Everyone is doing errands, and all sorts of other wonderful things, while I'm homebound."

"Do you need to go somewhere?" Mary Ellen asked, ready to retrace her steps.

"Not at all. I was just lonely, looking forward to your company as well as your advice." She led Mary into the dining room, where several pieces of jewelry lay on a beautifully finished teak table. The matching sideboard held an exotic Siamese headpiece, its small gold disks glittering as the silent ceiling fan ruffled the air. "These are a few of the pieces I'd like to have on film, but this time

I'd like to do something different. I want a man describing each piece in a voice that would curl a woman's toes. It will be *her* desire, not mine, that makes her buy."

Iris Mervyn had a vision, and it was up to Mary Ellen to make it a reality. She smiled. "I think I have someone who could fill that order," she lied, wondering which agency she could deliver the goods quickly and efficiently, without charging her a fortune.

"Good. He has to be friendly, yet sexy enough to stir a woman's heart. You know…a cross between Sean Connery and Mel Gibson. I want my customers to dream of men and diamonds when they hear my commercial. And not necessarily in that order."

Mary knew who would be perfect, but she doubted if Greg Torrance would care for the assignment. "I'll get on it this afternoon."

Mrs. Mervyn smiled like a Chesire cat. "Good. I'll write the script. That's the easy part."

"I'm glad you think so," Mary Ellen said with a wry grin.

Iris laughed and reached for a cigarette. "Well, it's either that or pay someone else to do it. Not that I'm taking it on because of the money. I can simply do it best."

It was the perfect opening. "Speaking of which, I understand you recommended me to Greg Torrance?"

"Greg?" The older woman gave a throaty laugh, her eyes twinkling in delight. "That's a plum I wish I could bake a pie for! And yes, I did. I've recommended you to others, too. Does that earn me a discount?''

Mary gave a shaky laugh. ''I already give you a discount.'' Her heart had skipped a beat as she'd recalled the warmth and intimacy of Greg's hand holding hers and the look in his eyes as he'd stared down at her. ''Greg Torrance is a charmer, isn't he?''

''You bet he is. He catches more flies with honey than most high-powered businessmen do with greenbacks. His ex-wife is a friend of mine, and his partner in the company. Even she says he can't be more fair, although there are times she'd love to choke him.''

''Not really,'' Mary protested, taking note of the ''ex'' before ''wife.''

''No. Not really. They've been partners since the very start. Although how Janet could be thrilled to work in that business is beyond me.'' Mrs. Mervyn gave a delicate shudder. ''I think what keeps them together is that neither of them could find anyone else with such a weird interest in magnetic pumps. That, and the fact that they still love each other.''

Mary's disappointment tasted like charcoal and sawdust. She should have known someone like Greg Torrance would be taken—if not physically, at least emotionally. It was a good thing she hadn't let herself get carried away with girlish dreams. She'd already been there and done that with the last man in her life. She would *not* go there again! Nor did she feel good about gossiping, but her curiosity was killing her. "Have they been in business a long time?"

"Ten years or so, I think. Greg bought the company a little after college graduation." Iris picked up a piece of jewelry and held it against the green velvet fabric bunched to one side of the table. "They attend many of the same social functions I do, so it's easy to keep up with them." She looked at Mary inquiringly. "Are you taking the job?"

"We're still negotiating." She couldn't help but think of all the bills she needed to pay next month, and how she wasn't exactly in a strong position to negotiate. She'd spent every dime to go into business now instead of waiting another five or ten years. The equipment alone had cost her over forty thousand dollars. Moreover, the thought of doing the job and showing him just how talented and capable she was would give her a great deal of satisfaction.

GREG WAS HEADING to a luncheon on busy Westheimer Boulevard when Mary Ellen Gallagher drove by, her gaze fixed on the road. He got that strange feeling in the pit of his stomach again, for reasons he didn't understand.

He was drawn to her, but that was no surprise. She was a terrific package—black hair, wide brown eyes and skin creamy enough to turn coffee blond. And those luscious lips... No. It was something about her personality...the fact that she was at once so capable and so vulnerable and so feminine.

Or maybe it was the fact that she seemed scared to get close to him and used words and body language to keep him at a distance. A challenge.

Or maybe it was plain old-fashioned chemistry.

Whatever it was, she'd gotten his full attention. And that was rare. She'd piqued his interest as no one had in years.

He had nothing to lose by finding out why.

2

MARY ELLEN PULLED INTO the driveway of her new money pit, a signed contract and a partial-payment check from Iris Mervyn in her briefcase.

Now if she could only close the deal with the Torrance Magnetic Pump Company the same way, she'd have a check four times larger than this one, with many more to come. Not only that, but the Torrance job could open doors to other companies that might need industrial videos and her expertise. Doing a good job for Torrance would establish her credentials in the industrial market.

She parked next to Edie's car.

Of course, all that was secondary to the *real* reason she wanted to do business with Greg Torrance. Bottom line was she wanted to prove what a great find he had made. She was a career woman—a talented career woman—who was able to make her own way in the world.

She opened the front door feeling so much better.

Edie was in the process of hanging up the phone. Grinning, she asked, "Guess who just confirmed a meeting with you?"

It took a lot to make Edie grin like that. "Greg Torrance?" Mary Ellen guessed.

"Greg Torrance."

Mary's heart skipped a beat and she had to fight down a grin that would have matched Edie's. "For what?"

Edie looked blank. "What do you mean, 'for what'? What has he been wanting all along? He wants you to do his video."

"We're not sure about that yet." Mary said it more to keep her own hopes down than to tamp down Edie's.

"Speak for yourself. I am as sure as I've ever been."

Mary Ellen dropped her briefcase on her desk and sat on the edge. "What did he say, exactly?"

"He was confirming your appointment."

"And?"

Edie looked smug. "And I think he's interested in more than business, if you know what I mean."

Mary's stomach fluttered. "You're dreaming."

"I'm wide-awake, and you should get that way, too, for heaven's sake. It's about time you put that last fiasco behind you. At least this guy is a grown man with a real life."

Mary brushed away reminders of that horrible time in her life, unwilling to let those memories dampen her mood. "He's probably got every female he meets falling at his feet. I won't be one of them." She picked up the stack of mail and skimmed through it. "Besides, he's not looking for a relationship. He's still madly in love with his ex-wife.''

Edie looked stunned. Then disgusted. ''Damn, I thought I could spot a lecher a mile away, but this one slipped through my defenses.''

''What are you talking about?'' Mary demanded, shocked by Edie's passionate response.

''Mr. Torrance,'' Edie replied. ''He must be one of those stuck-on-himself kinda guys. You know the type. Good-looking, great businessman, all 'round Mr. Nice Guy. But underneath, he's the kind of creep who drags innocent but inflamed women through the mud and back, and doesn't even say so much as 'thank you for your troubles and the rug burns on your buns.'''

Mary laughed out loud. Edie had made her point. And Mary realized she *was* probably jumping to conclusions about Greg Torrance. Feeling silly, she stood and gave a sigh. ''Well, don't feel bad, Edie. We were both wrong.''

''If I were you,'' Edie replied, ''I wouldn't meet with the man. He might try the old casting-couch routine, and then where would you be? Drinking fine champagne, eating caviar and making love in the afternoon in his high-rise office with a view of the whole city. My God, perish the thought! You might actually *enjoy* it! *Tsk, tsk, tsk.*''

Ignoring the digs, Mary stood and looked over her assistant's shoulder at the open appointment book. ''So when *is* this meeting?''

"You mean you're going to take a chance with this emotionally scarred man?"

"Don't worry. I'm armed and dangerous myself. I'm going to dazzle him with my business acumen and then wow him with my talent *behind* the camera."

Edie almost looked crestfallen. "Maybe his good looks won't blind *you*, but I'm buying sunglasses! And you'll still have to beware of his great attributes and vital personality."

"Okay," Mary finally admitted. "So I find him attractive. I'm still not going into a relationship unless the circumstances are perfect. I'm not, repeat not, some sort of therapist for wayward men who can't seem to get their adult acts together. But…I'll still do business with him if I can."

"I don't blame you. Take away his good looks and personality, and the guy's still worth a mint and wants the best for his money. That's you. Just because the rest of the world hasn't yet beaten a path to your doorstep doesn't mean they won't later. You're damn good. And that's why you have an appointment with Mr. Greg Torrance at his plant at nine o'clock tomorrow morning."

"Ah," Mary said with a contented sigh. "That's it. Stroke my ego and you've got job security forever." She grinned. "Don't worry. I wouldn't miss this opportunity for the world. And my bill collectors wouldn't have it any other way."

MARY ENTERED the plush executive secretary's area, butterflies going wild in her stomach. Stiffly, she delivered a smile, for the third time, to a secretary, hoping this was the last in the series before she actually got to see their boss.

She'd worn her best suit, royal blue with one large mother-of-pearl button on the jacket at the waist. Her blouse was white silk and tailored. She wore her tallest heels—of black alligator skin—and a matching purse. The outfit made her feel like the executive she wanted to be.

She walked up to the desk. "Hi, I have a nine o'clock appointment with Mr. Torrance."

The older woman looked up and answered her smile. "You must be Ms. Gallagher. He'll be right back. He's on the assembly line right now, checking out a press that won't do what it's supposed to do when it's supposed to do it."

"Sounds like a major problem," Mary murmured, looking around for a seat.

"Not for Greg. Or for Janet, either, actually." The woman nodded toward one of the two closed doors between which her desk sat. "They both seem to have an uncanny ability to talk to those machines."

There was a deep chuckle, and then a voice responded, "They only answer when I remember my manners."

Mary and the secretary both turned toward Greg Torrance, who stood at the entrance to the waiting area. He was dressed in a pair of gray suit pants coupled with a white dress shirt and tie. His shirtsleeves were rolled up to just below his elbows, his forearms as bronzed and muscled as Mary had imagined they would be. He held his jacket with a crooked finger over one shoulder.

"Hello, Ms. Gallagher," he said in a low, husky tone of voice that teased her senses. "Good to see you again."

"Hello, Mr. Torrance," she replied, kicking herself for sounding like a schoolmarm, sounding as uptight as she felt. As she followed him into the office, she silently gave herself a pep talk.

"Keep the masses out for a few minutes, will you, Suzanne?" he called over his shoulder.

"They'll have to use a battering ram, boss," she said cheerily, her nose in the air as she peered through a pair of bright yellow bifocals. She never missed a keystroke. "'Cept, of course, if the presses break down again."

"Of course," he agreed before quietly closing the door. He leaned against the frame and stared at Mary.

Today his eyes were more blue than green, and his gaze made her feel taut and tense and very aware of her own movements.

She walked around his office, her fingers trailing across the furniture she passed. The scent of the room assailed her first; it was a mixture of rich leather, aftershave, ink and pencil shavings, giving the overall impression of a very male working atmosphere. Instead of the expensive, showy office she'd expected, she found a large, utilitarian workroom. There was a conference table at one end covered with several large sets of blueprints and stacks of paper. At the opposite end of the room was an enormous desk equally buried by plans. Two dark green leather easy chairs across from Greg's desk were the only pieces of furniture free of papers.

Greg finally eased away from the door and threw his jacket over one of the chairs. "Alone at last."

Her eyes widened warily, but he hadn't waited to see her response. Instead, he followed her path, came around his desk and sat in one of the big leather chairs, rocking in an easy motion.

Taking a seat in the other chair, Mary sat primly on the edge and waited, her briefcase next to her.

He gave another sigh and began rolling down one shirtsleeve. "Okay, Ms. Gallagher. I can't seem to get you to lighten up. What say we get to the bottom line?"

She was so nervous she barely kept her insides from shaking. "I *am* lightened up and ready to get to that bottom line," she said with a steel thread of determination in her voice. At least *that* didn't quiver. She reached for her briefcase.

Holding out his hand like a traffic cop, Greg stopped her. "Let's try again," he said. "Let's talk first."

Her hands stilled on the snap locks, the flesh around her nails turning white from her grip. Knowing she desperately needed the money his business would bring, Mary tried not to show any emotion.

Instead, she withdrew into chilliness. "Just last week, Mr. Torrance, you told me that you were ready to sign immediately. I was the one who asked you to wait."

"Are you certain this is what *you* want to do?" he retorted.

She was surprised he would ask. "Of course it is. Why?"

"Because suddenly you won't look me in the eye. You act as if I've got the plague and you can't even make small talk." He leaned forward. "What is it, Mary Ellen Gallagher? What is it about me that turns you off?"

"Nothing," she whispered.

Silence hung in the air. His eyes delved into hers; he was waiting for an answer.

How could she tell him she'd been drawn to him from the beginning and felt as if she needed to pull back, even when nothing had gone on between them? She wouldn't take the chance of dreaming about a man ever again. She wasn't ready for any more hurt, and he looked as if he could give her plenty of that.

She gave herself a shake mentally. It all sounded so silly. So much reaction for a simple meeting.

But somehow he had touched her emotionally, and she resented the fact that she had allowed it to happen. She wasn't angry with him. She was angry with herself!

Just then a blond woman in a pair of overalls and an expensive white silk blouse appeared at the door. "Hi, how's it going?"

Greg reacted as if it was the most natural thing in the world to find a woman at his door in overalls and silk. For him, it probably was. "I'm trying to talk Ms. Gallagher into relaxing in my presence, but it's a no go. Maybe *you* can put her at ease."

The woman stepped forward and walked to Mary Ellen's side, holding out her hand. "Hi, I'm Janet Torrance," she said, looking friendly and open as she shook Mary's hand. "And you're the one Iris Mervyn and a few other people call the talented lady with the camera."

Mary smiled. "You've heard of me?"

"Of course," Janet said easily. "Greg told me he saw several of your videos and thinks you're extremely talented. He showed me a sample, and I agree." She grinned impishly and gave her ex-husband a knowing look. Her straight blond bob shimmered in the sunlight as she looked back at Mary Ellen. "Greg and I both prefer to hire women whenever we can. I'm also for anything that makes us money. You working on this project sounds like a wonderful combination of my favorite things."

"In case you haven't noticed, Mary Ellen, Janet is a card-carrying feminist." Greg said indulgently by way of explanation. It was the first time he'd ever said her name, and she fell silent, watching the easy rapport shared by Greg Torrance and his ex-wife. She was envying them their comradery when Janet turned to Mary. "What do you think?" she asked. "Are good jobs easy to find?"

"No. Not even if you're the best," Mary answered quickly. "If you're not the best, you're lost."

Janet smiled smugly. "And you're the best."

Mary made no apologies. "Yes, I am. And I've proven it to every one of my clients." So, she'd only had five clients since she opened her business, it wasn't necessary to mention that. Not necessary at all.

Laughing, Janet crossed her arms and leaned against Greg's desk. "Well, I'm all in favor. When does she start?"

"As soon as Ms. Gallagher and I agree on the terms. Right now, she seems to view me as some kind of uncivilized monster and can't relax long enough to talk to me."

"Ms. Gallagher can speak for herself," Mary Ellen stated, finally finding the nerve to speak up, but not willing to admit to his claim. "I'm not frightened, I'm just not certain that I'm the right one for the job."

"And what would it take to convince you otherwise?" Greg asked.

"Magnetic pumps might be one of the few things that need a man's slant."

"I'll give it to you. You video it."

"Or I'll give you a female slant," Janet said.

Why was she fighting this? Mary Ellen wondered. She needed the work, wanted the job and liked the people. What was the holdup? Greg was a friendly man who seemed just as genuine now as he had in her kitchen. "Let me get the contract and you can sign on the dotted line while we all think it's a good idea," she said, reaching for her briefcase one more time.

Janet pulled away from the desk. "Well, my job's done. I'll leave you two to the final deed. I've got a shipment for Exxon to get out."

Greg leaned back in his chair. "Thanks. Talk to you later."

"Don't forget the board meeting tomorrow afternoon."

"As you leave, would you please ask Suzanne to remind me again tomorrow?"

"Yes, Greg," Janet replied in a singsong voice. She left the room, her arm raised behind her. "Bye-bye."

Once more silence invaded the large office. "She's lovely," Mary finally said.

"Yes, she is." His tone was quiet. Matter-of-fact. He sat silently, patiently, waiting for her next move.

"Were you married long?" she asked brightly, still fumbling with the lock on her briefcase.

"I see you heard the gossip," he said, his voice a little tight. "Let me answer some of your unasked questions so we can get it behind us. I don't want it brought up later, at a more sensitive time."

"But—"

Greg continued in a monotone as if she'd never spoken. "We were married when we were eighteen, went through college together. We divorced almost two years ago because Janet decided she needed to fall in love and experience all the chaos that went with it. We have one child—a son, Jason—and we are still best friends." His blue-gray eyes pierced Mary Ellen's. "Anything else you want to know?"

With each of his words, her secret hopes were dashed against the rock of truth. The man she was attracted to was divorced but still in love with his ex-wife. Too much baggage. Too close to home. Too close to a repeat of her experience with Joe just two years ago.

"I think you've covered it all," Mary said, leaning back and lifting one eyebrow as if she was unconcerned. "It's really nice that both of you have an interest in the same business." Opening her briefcase and pulling out the duplicate contracts Edie had prepared earlier, she slid them across the desk to his waiting hand.

Greg began signing, and without looking up, he replied, "It is." When he finished, he shoved the papers toward her. "In short, Janet is my best friend, my partner in the company and, as of two years ago, my ex-wife, because no one can really have it all."

Mary Ellen wouldn't ask what that meant. It didn't matter. She believed she could have it all, and Greg's signature on the contract helped underline the fact. As long as she kept distance between them, she'd do fine.

Mary signed both copies then handed his back. "So you're legally divorced."

"Yes, divorced. Legally." A frown marred his forehead. "So, we're both single."

Mary felt frustration building inside. She needed to backtrack, fast. She didn't *want* to know more about his personal life. "I didn't mean to pry. It's just that I was wondering if Janet needs to sign the agreement, too." Mary looked at his bold signature on the bottom of the contract.

She stuck the contract in her briefcase, clicked it shut and stood. She held out her hand. "The law gives you three days to change your mind about this contract. When you're ready, please give me a call and we can discuss the next phase of the film."

Greg stood, but he didn't accept her hand. "You're still afraid of me."

There was no sense denying it. They both knew he was discussing their mutual attraction. "Yes, I am."

"Why?"

"Because you're a charmer, Mr. Torrance. And if I don't miss my guess, you didn't really want the divorce. Plus, I like your wife."

"My ex-wife," he automatically corrected. "And if you didn't?"

"It still stands. You're still a charmer and

you're still married—at least emotionally," she said firmly.

"You're a wise woman, Ms. Gallagher."

"Yes, I am."

"You're also wrong."

She shook her head for emphasis. "No, I'm not. Believe me, I've learned what's good for me and what's not."

"And I'm not good for you?"

"Not on a personal level," she finally admitted, dropping her outstretched hand and heading for the door. She couldn't believe she'd said that aloud. It had been a thought barely born and now it was out in the open.

Greg looked smug. "At least you acknowledge we both know there's something flaring between us."

Her chin lifted a notch higher. "It doesn't matter. Nothing will happen."

"We'll have to see about that, Ms. Gallagher. We'll just see." Greg Torrance's soft, deep voice was filled with determination.

So was her heart.

3

WHEN MARY ELLEN AWOKE the next morning, she didn't move. Instead, she stared at the peeling paint on the ceiling, thinking about the day before, going over every detail. Greg Torrance had laughed and enjoyed his ex-wife's presence.

Most men didn't have that kind of relationship with their ex-wives. She'd known men who called their ex-partner derogatory names, and she'd known men who pined over their lost love like mooning children, discussing their version of the breakup with anyone who would sit still long enough to listen.

But not Greg Torrance. He'd brought his old flame in to meet the woman he was thinking of dating. Not that he had asked for a date yet. But Mary could read the signs. She knew he was interested; their conversation had confirmed it.

She kept telling herself that this film deal was strictly business. No more, no less. She grinned, thinking about the signed contract in her briefcase. In three days, she'd have enough money in the bank to pay for three months of Edie's salary and four months on the mortgage. She'd be able to bring some past-due bills up-to-date. And *that* was just one-quarter of the total amount she would earn when this job was done.

She wouldn't have been so hard-pressed for money if she hadn't had to buy her way out of a five-year contract with her last boss. He was a movie producer who had left that field and gone into industrial films, becoming one of the top names in the country. In the beginning she'd thought she would have artistic license to do her work while learning even more under his tutelage. But when he took one of her films and won a top award for it under his own name, she learned he'd done that with other apprentices, too. She did everything she could to claim ownership, but it was no use. According to the contract, any work done in his company was his, period. As a consolation, her name appeared in small print as one of the many who had worked on the project. That was hard to swallow, because until she'd finished the film, he'd never seen it.

One month later, she withdrew all her savings from the bank, took out a loan, paid off her contract and left. Edie went with her. Even though she'd get fewer hours and less pay, she'd said she wanted the opportunity to grow with Mary Ellen. Edie believed that Mary would one day have a major company of her own.

Though she couldn't really afford it, she hadn't been about to pass up the opportunity to get state-of-the-art equipment at a relatively cheap price while she still had credit to use. And then the house, which belonged to a friend, had fallen into her lap. So now she was starting business in the hole—a big hole.

But she'd make it. She was good and she knew it. All she had to do was convince people like Greg Torrance.

Her mind whirled with filming possibilities, ways to explain the pump business. She needed time to figure out what would be the best angle, but she'd do it.

Ever since she could remember, she'd seen things—people, situations, life in general—as if through a camera lens. With or without a camera in her hands, she'd always mentally set up shots that would tell a story, filling in the dialogue in her head. In those dreamlike moments, she'd said all the right things, walked out all the right doors at the right times. In the constantly playing movies in her head, she'd done everything right.

It was a shame she hadn't done so well in real life. Her thoughts led her, as they often did, to Joe. When she'd met him three years ago in a photo supplier's warehouse, she'd been instantly attracted, and he'd felt the same way—or so it had seemed. He was a student of still photography at one of the major art schools. They'd struck up a conversation while she was waiting for her supplies to be boxed. The next time she went back, he was there again, and this time they walked across the parking lot to a fast-food restaurant and talked over a soft drink. That was the beginning of what she'd thought would be the love of her life. Before it was over she'd lost everything but her self-respect.

He'd wooed her into giving her heart to him. Then came the emotional game playing: he dangled the prize of marriage and children in front of her while saying he wasn't sure he was ready. He boyishly confessed that, as soon as he *was* ready, their marriage would be wonderful and special. All she had to do was wait...and in the meantime play house as if they really were married so he could be convinced that it would work out.

She was never sure why but she agreed to the arrangement, even though living together out of wedlock was against everything she believed in. But she told herself she loved him and that once he saw just how wonderful and special it would be with her as a life mate, he would change his mind. They played house for over a year, but very slowly she realized there was something missing. Something wonderful and special. Their relationship deteriorated until shortly after their year anniversary of living together, Joe was coming home only to sleep. Mary Ellen finally gave him an ultimatum: that they get married or break up.

Reluctantly, Joe agreed to marriage. Certain that he would become more enthusiastic after the ceremony, she continued with the wedding plans. She put down money on a hall, ordered flowers and food and bought a gown that she hoped would be an heirloom for their children.

She did it all alone and at a feverish pitch, trying to arrange the perfect affair.

The night before the event, Joe came home drunk and crying. It was then that he'd confessed he was still in love—and secretly seeing—his old girlfriend, who now lived in Austin. She and Joe had broken up three months before he'd met Mary Ellen, but when they'd run into each other again, they'd found the attraction was still there. In fact, there was a chance his old girlfriend wanted him back permanently. Joe said he was sorry for hurting Mary but that he'd never stopped loving his girlfriend, and whatever he felt for Mary wasn't enough to make him stay.

Unbelieving and in a panic, Mary had pleaded with him to realize what he was throwing away. Still, he'd remained unmoved. Mary was stung into silence for all of a minute. Then the anger flowed, swift and strong and sure.

She told him off in every term she could think of. He accepted his blame, then calmly asked her to pay the remainder of her share of the rent, saying it was okay with him if she stayed until the end of the month. Then he'd left her to clean up the mess and driven off for a weekend in Austin, late for a date with his beloved.

With an icy heart, Mary had called everyone on the guest list and all the vendors, letting them know that the wedding was off. That done, she'd packed her belongings. She had taken time to straighten up the apartment, which held only a few things that were hers. Any items that couldn't fit into the car she left behind.

Her last act was to dial the time and temperature…in Austin. Leaving the receiver and her key on the counter, she had left the apartment.

It was the end of the relationship, but not the end of the pain—or the shame. She had to listen to all her friends expounding on her sorrow. She had to hear what she should have known earlier—that all the signs had been there, but she'd been too blinded by love to pay attention.

Rolling over in bed, Mary gave a heavy sigh. Oh yes, she knew what pain Greg Torrance could cause her. She knew how it was to be in love with someone who didn't love you back. Feeling used and soiled, somehow, and very, very stupid was awful, and she never, *never* wanted to be in that position again.

Never.

That meant she had to ignore the fluttering in her stomach and the way her heart beat when she was near him. She had to focus on enjoying a casual acquaintance and a profitable business association. For her own sake, she *had* to refocus.

She could do that.

She really could.

GREG TIGHTENED THE KNOT in his tie, finally satisfied with his efforts. He had a board meeting and he wanted a certain look—he needed to be as intimidating as possible. Today was the day that he informed the board about hiring Mary Ellen

Gallagher for the promo film and took a vote on his decision. He was determined to get a majority vote.

He looked forward to seeing Mary and giving her the check to start the film rolling.

He told himself it was because of her house. Judging from the renovations required, he'd say she needed all the help she could get. She also tackled anything in her path with the gusto of someone who enjoyed life and living. Greg admired that. But the truth was, he admitted, she excited him in other ways, and he'd been living in an emotional vacuum for too long.

He wasn't sure exactly *what* he was feeling about Mary, but that didn't matter, he told himself. After he and Janet broke up, it was as if all his emotions had been plunged into a deep freeze, and they'd stayed there for a very long time. Apparently, he was now part of the living again, and he was damn well going to enjoy it.

MARY ELLEN FINISHED dubbing in the music for an industrial film she'd made last week for a small T-shirt factory. It was the last step in the editing process, and, technically, the easiest. The camera snapped from one smiling employee to another, everyone was wearing the product. She'd chosen an upbeat tempo for the background music and now all she had to do was keep the music in sync with the images on film.

Several tedious hours later, she took off her headset, leaned back and stretched her arms over her head, relaxing her shoulders with a satisfied sigh. Then she heard a call that immediately made her tense up again.

"Mary Ellen? Are you there?" Greg's deep voice echoed through the house.

"In the studio behind the office," she called back, trying to gather herself together. She heard his footsteps on the wooden floor before he appeared in the doorway.

"Is this the Land of Genius?" he asked, giving her a wide, sexy smile.

"But of course," she said, laying the headset on the console and allowing the happiness she felt at seeing him to show through. She just couldn't help it, and it wasn't a sin to enjoy his company.... "The magic occurs here."

Greg took in the vast array of electronic gadgets filling a six-foot wall. He zeroed in on the console with all its dials and knobs. "What's going on now?"

Mary studied her equipment, seeing it through his eyes. She was proud of the studio she'd managed to put together. Most of it wasn't paid for yet, of course, but she had bought some of it used and had bartered for other pieces. All in all it was equipment anyone in the video business would envy. "With VHS tape, video is separate from audio. You can alter sound and picture independently."

Greg tilted his head, dropping his gaze from the console to her. "And that explains what you're doing here this late in the evening?"

Mary Ellen nodded. "I've been inserting background music behind the voice-over we taped yesterday." She flipped several switches and shut down the main computer. "I'm done."

"I'm impressed."

She laughed. "You're supposed to be. After all, you just hired me."

Greg shook his head. "No, I'm impressed with your equipment. I might never have seen this equipment if I hadn't come over so late."

Feeling vaguely insulted, Mary stood and clicked off the small banker's lamp that sat on the edge of the console. "Which reminds me, why are you here?" He followed her back through the office and into the hallway. "Cup of tea?" she asked, nodding toward the kitchen. She was going to fix some anyway, she told herself, and he was already here...for whatever reason.

"We didn't finish our board meeting until after five," Greg was explaining. "I wanted to get the check to you right away, so you'd know we're not changing our minds. We want you to film the video. But one thing led to another, and the time got away from me."

"We?" Mary asked casually. She filled the dented metal teakettle and set it on the old stove to boil, as if she didn't feel like jumping up and down with joy. A check! It was real now, not just a happy thought.

"The board of directors. We met all afternoon, going over a few of the sticky things that boards of directors go over."

"Sounds…boring," she admitted.

"It is. But it's necessary. Besides," he joked, "it brought me back to you—with a check. Or does that sound boring, too?"

She couldn't repress a grin. "And just exactly where is this alleged check?"

He reached into his vest pocket and pulled out an envelope. "Right here."

Her smile lit up the room. "Thank you."

"You're welcome."

"Not that I don't deserve it, you understand. I do great work…" she said, looking everywhere but at Greg.

"Mary Ellen," he said quietly.

"If you doubt my ability, I can give you more examples of work I've done in the past—"

"Mary," he said again, this time in a voice laced with steel.

She finally looked up. "Yes?"

"You've already sold me, remember? I already signed the contract. I'm already your client."

"I know, but you seemed to have some doubts." She looked at him then, took in every nuance. Cautiously, she said, "I'm just making sure you're happy with our deal."

"I'm happy." His frown belied his words. "You're the one who seems to lack confidence in this deal. What is it about the project that bothers you?"

"Bothers me? Nothing." She pulled the whistling kettle off the stove and poured water into the teapot, glad for the chance to look away. She didn't want him to know this was the biggest job she'd ever handled—not until it was successfully completed. "Well, I feel I should know more about pumps. Magnetic and otherwise."

"I can get you all the information you'll need." Greg eased himself down into one of the wooden kitchen chairs and stared at her. "Now, what else is bothering you?"

"Nothing. You've answered all my questions." Her answer was more brisk than she'd meant it to be, but she wasn't sure how to act. This was uncertain ground. He was a client, but she was drawn to him personally. He was all-business, but it was after hours. She was a professional, and what she felt was crazy....

Suddenly, she realized he'd been speaking. "Excuse me?"

"I asked when your contractor was going to start work on the electricity?" he repeated.

Mary glanced around at the extension cords draped across the kitchen and blushed. "I know it looks awful, but most clients don't see this part of the house. You just happened to come back right from the get-go."

"Don't get defensive," Greg soothed. "I'm only asking because I know there's so much more to it than installing an outlet."

"I know that, but…"

"And the cord you're using right now is made to handle a lamp, not a microwave or a toaster."

Mary squinted at the brown cord. "How do you know?"

"Because I'm an electrical engineer, remember? Look here, the cord has a UL approval on the end that tells you what it's good for. Anything more than its maximum, and you can call out 'fire' just about anytime."

Mary moved closer, trying to read the small print on the end of the cord. "Are you sure?"

The sound of Greg's deep laugh touched something inside her. She didn't feel hurt or angry or even foolish. She felt good having made him laugh.

"I'm sure," he said. "And if something isn't done quickly, you'll fry all that expensive equipment in your office."

Her mind whirled at the possibility. Could she afford to do the electrical work and still make the payments on her equipment? She smiled sheepishly. "I'm afraid I didn't pay much attention to the cords when I picked them up. I just grabbed a handful and ran to the register. But I did remember to buy some really good power surgers for the equipment."

Just as she spoke, the refrigerator motor hummed and the lights dimmed in response.

"That's a sign, Mary," Greg cautioned. "You need to rehaul the electrical system first. Otherwise, everything's going to go up in smoke… literally."

"You're right." She sighed, suddenly feeling overwhelmed and totally out of her element. She pushed a wayward strand of dark hair behind one ear. "But you see, I haven't had time to learn how to rewire things yet. It's my next priority, but..." She gave a shrug. How could she explain that not even working twenty hours a day was bringing in the capital she'd need to pay for a master electrician? How did she admit that, while *she* knew she was good, the rest of the world hadn't caught on to that fact yet? That Greg's account was the largest she'd handled on her own?

Greg smiled and she almost forgot what she was worrying about. "Why don't we make a deal?" he proposed. "I'm itching to see if I still remember how to do hands-on work, and you need an electrician as soon as possible, no questions. So hire me."

As if on cue, the lights dimmed again, but this time the refrigerator *didn't* kick on. Mary Ellen realized it must have something to do with the fans on her electronic equipment. If anything happened to that...

Greg looked serious and thoughtful, but his steel blue eyes held a definite twinkle that said he saw an opportunity and knew what to do with it. "I'm cheap and I can start tomorrow afternoon."

"What is cheap?" she asked cautiously.

Greg gave a heavy sigh. "Electrical parts and lots of tea and cookies—served at the times I'm available instead of the normal nine to five."

Mary grinned, her heart lighting up as much as her smile. "You've got a deal, Mr. Torrance," she said, reaching out her hand for a shake.

Greg took her hand between both of his, and

instead of pumping it up and down, he rubbed his callused fingers against her softer skin. "I'll start tomorrow afternoon. Is that all right with you?"

She swallowed to wet her dry throat. "Fine. If I'm not here, Edie will be. I'll let her know."

Greg's eyes narrowed as he studied her. "Will it bother you if I'm working here in the evening?"

She swallowed again, her gaze not able to meet his right away. But when she did, she stared without flinching. "Will it bother *you*?"

He let go of her hand and reached for the teacup, a wry smile on his lips. "More than you know, but it will be worth it." He gulped down the last of his tea, then stood. "At least I won't be so worried about your house burning down with you in it."

"Why? Why would you be worried about me?" she asked. "You have a wife and child you love. You have a business you seem to wallow in willingly. And you have one of the top companies of its kind in the country." She couldn't keep her curiosity to herself any longer. "Why me?"

Greg hesitated only a second. "Because I'm fascinated with you. Don't ask me any more than that, Mary, because I don't think I could answer. All I can say is that you're an enticing woman." At the gleam in his eyes, Mary Ellen flushed. "And mighty tempting."

She didn't know what to do, faced with this

blatantly sexual male animal. She'd never run into his kind before.

"And that's why you're willing to do electrical work for nothing?"

"No, that's why I *want* to do your electrical. I think we could be really good friends, Mary Ellen Gallagher. And I want to test that theory." His smile was slow in coming, but so darn beautiful it heated Mary's whole body. "My mama used to say you can never have enough friends."

She kept her face straight as an ironing board. "My mama used to say beware of men with silver tongues—you wind up spending a lot of time polishing."

Greg's laughter was her reward.

"See what I mean?" he finally asked. "Most women would be telling me off or cozying up to me. But not you, Mary. You give as good as you get."

She stood, her smile matching his, her insides heated with his compliment. "Thank you, I think."

"You're welcome," he answered. "I'm sure."

She stiffened her spine against his charm. "You do understand that this is just a friendly deal, don't you?"

"I understand," he repeated softly. "And whatever happens in the future, Mary, it will be with full consent from both of us. And if I work at changing your mind and turning this into a more, uh, intimate relationship, it's still your call."

There was a promise in his voice that made her heart speed up. She wasn't sure she could handle him, but she wanted the chance to try. ''Thank you.''

They walked to the door silently. When Mary opened it, Greg stopped and faced her directly, his gaze holding hers, his mouth just inches from her own. Her limbs felt paralyzed; she was unable to move.

Finally, with agonizing slowness, he bent and his lips brushed hers. Once. Twice. Then they brushed again and stayed. Her breath caught in her throat. She wanted to feel his body pressed against her; instinctively she arched her spine in anticipation.

To her disappointment, Greg pulled away. ''Good night, Mary Ellen,'' he said as he stepped over the threshold. ''Lock the door behind me. It's dangerous out here.'' He stepped over the threshold.

She did as she was told and slammed the door.

He'd had no right to kiss her!

He had no right to lead her on!

But as she marched up the stairs to her bedroom, all she could think of was what it might have been like to complete that kiss.

He'd been wrong about the danger being outside. Tonight, for her, it had been far more dangerous inside....

MARY'S DAY WAS SHAPING UP to be as busy as her mind had been all night—which was nothing new.

First thing, Edie had handed her fourteen demo tapes of men reading for Iris Mervyn's commercial. Mary Ellen spent most of the morning listening to male voices, keeping in mind the effect Iris wanted. The tapes had come from various agents she and Edie had called, but by noon, still no luck. But that didn't mean the next one wouldn't be just right.

Edie had been on the phone most of the morning soliciting business. She always followed up leads, and even rumors; sometimes it paid off. Ever organized, Edie had taken on sales, marketing and organization, bless her, and left Mary to the creative work.

It was late afternoon before Mary Ellen and Edie put their feet on Mary Ellen's desk and ate sandwiches delivered by a gawky kid from their local deli.

"So you got the Torrance check. I suppose that means you can funnel more money into the house now...to say nothing of my pocket."

Edie took a huge bite of her sandwich, and Mary wondered how such a tiny woman could wolf down goodies the way Edie did.

"I'm writing you a check tonight. Not only that..." Mary paused to sip her iced tea "...I've also got a master electrician to help make sense of this wiring mess, hopefully *before* my equipment explodes."

"I'm glad. I didn't say anything, but I was a

little worried myself." Edie sheepishly ducked
under the desk and pulled out a small fire extin-
guisher. "I even bought one of these, just in
case...."

"Why didn't you say something?" Mary admonished. "I had no idea you felt so insecure!"

"Well, I did. I also knew how short money's
been. Running a business on bank loans isn't
easy." Edie shrugged. "But it's getting better already! When's the electrician coming?"

"Tonight." Mary calmly took another bite of
her sandwich. Her heart beat faster just from saying the word.

"Tonight?" Edie's eyes narrowed. "What kind
of master electrician works at night?"

"A cheap one," Mary said, finally allowing a
grin to burst through. "Greg Torrance wants to
do the wiring. To keep his hand in," she explained.

Edie looked stunned. "To keep his hand in
what?"

Mary blushed. "In working with electrical sys-
tems. And he says he loves to putter."

"I knew that the moment I saw him," Edie
swore, tongue in cheek. "I just thought he loved
to putter with something besides electricity."

"Cut that out," Mary Ellen admonished. "He
offered and I accepted. No hanky-panky. Nothing but friendship. You can't have too many
friends...."

"I'll say." Edie finished her sandwich and
dusted her lap of crumbs. Her gaze was delving,

seeking. "And you realize that this man is very—I said *very*—interested in you?"

Mary started to deny it, then thought better. "I know."

"And that he wants a relationship with you? And you do recall you've only just stopped bouncing off walls from the last horror story?"

A shiver raced down Mary Ellen's spine. "Joe has been gone a long time, Edie," she said quietly. "But the lesson he taught me is branded on my heart and in my head. I won't be forgetting quickly, if ever."

"Then why are you opening yourself to this man?" Edie asked. "I know how sexy he is. I thought so from the moment I saw him. And he's got enough money to show you how the other half lives. But do you really think you're capable of having a good time and walking away, heart intact?"

"We're strictly friends, Edie." Mary chose to ignore the quickening in her pulse at the guilty memory of his lips touching hers. "We discussed it and we agreed that we'd be just friends. We'll both abide by that decision."

"Isn't that like the hungry alligator giving the monkey a ride across the river? As I recall, one of them was eaten before they reached the banks."

"I'm not a monkey," Mary Ellen said, tossing the remnants of her lunch in the trash can.

Edie cocked a knowing brow. "Maybe not, but my guess is Greg Torrance didn't get where he is today without having a lot of the hungry alligator in him."

Mary knew when to keep her mouth shut and her opinions to herself. "Who knows?" she responded, leaving her desk and heading back to the studio. She'd promised to edit an employee-picnic video for a local plumbing business.

But the entire time she was editing, the image of Greg Torrance as a hungry alligator drifted across her mind's eye. And he would be here tonight.

4

MARY'S STOMACH FLUTTERED as she opened the front door to Greg. He stood on the porch holding two brown paper bags.

"Beware of Greeks bearing gifts," he said as he led the way back to the kitchen. "Although I'm not Greek, so I guess you can let me in."

She peered over his arm to peep into the bag. "What have you got in there?"

"A menu fit for a king—or a very hungry woman."

He set the bags down in the kitchen table, and when Mary started to investigate the first bag, he snagged her wrist, making her a gentle captive. "Not until I'm ready to serve. Sit your pretty butt down and wait like a lady is supposed to." His mischievous grin was contagious.

"If I was a lady, I would throw you out for being so high-handed, mister." Standing with her chin tilted for war, she added, "But, thank goodness for you, I'm not a lady. I'm a working-woman who needs nourishment."

With that, she dived into the food as if she hadn't had a bite to eat all day. And she purposely ignored the attraction between them, which was very nearly palpable.

THEY WERE WORKING on an outlet in the office when Greg began asking questions.

"Does your family live around here?" he asked, stripping an old wire.

"No. My dad died when I was a teenager. Mom died almost two years ago. There's just me and my two sisters left."

"The Gallagher girls, huh?"

She smiled. "The Gallagher girls." She'd heard that all her life. "That's us."

"Are you the oldest?"

"I'm in the middle."

"Where do your sisters live?"

Mary Ellen smiled as she thought of her siblings. When she was younger she'd dreamed of getting away from being one of the Gallagher girls, and beginning a "grown-up" life of her own. Strangely, the older she got the more she missed them. "Virginia lives in Austin," she said. "She's a chef. Elizabeth, lovingly known to the family as Betty Jean, lives outside of Atlanta, Georgia. She works with pregnant teens."

"Are you still in touch with them?"

"Yes. But not nearly enough. When I moved to Houston, I honestly thought I'd get a chance to see Virginia more often, but I haven't gotten up to see her more than a dozen times in the past four years."

He looked over his shoulder at her. "Why not invite her down?"

Mary's eyes widened. "She's got a full-time catering firm, a husband who owns a major company and a baby."

His laughter was low and sensuous. "Doesn't everybody? Invite her anyway."

"Sure," she said, but her voice had dropped to a whisper. "Next time I talk to her, I'll do that."

His gaze never wavered from her face. "You should call your other sister, too—Betty Jean. Invite her down for a vacation."

Mary licked dry lips and swallowed. "I've tried. She'll take anything that has to do with her job—pregnant girls, teenage fathers-to-be, angry parents—but she's scared to take a vacation."

With longing plainly visible in the depths of his sexy eyes, Greg said, "You've got the most beautiful mouth I've ever seen."

"Unfair," she whispered as warmth infused her whole body, melting her insides like hot wax.

She watched his own sensuous mouth slowly move as he answered, "Unfair to whom?"

Every fiber of her being cried out for him to kiss her. She craved the pressure of his lips, the taste of his tongue, the feel of his face against her cheek. She wanted his arms around her, firmly holding her, keeping her body anchored. She wanted…

A deep, regretful sigh on his lips, Greg turned away and paid attention once more to the wire in his hand. "Let me have the screwdriver, will you?"

Traitor! Tease! Furious and frustrated, she plucked the screwdriver from the tool case at her side and slapped it into his hand. Standing up, she turned on her heel and strode into the hallway.

"Hey," Greg called. "Where's my helper?"

"I don't know," she called over her shoulder, irritation growing with every moment spent in his company. "If you need one, hire one, then bill me!" By the time she reached the kitchen and poured herself a cup of tea, she was fuming.

He'd been toying with her! He'd done that on purpose, getting her all worked up and then pretending nothing had happened. He'd planned the whole—

Holding a screwdriver in his hand, Greg walked into the kitchen. "What's going on?" he asked innocently. "Did I upset you?"

Mary stiffened. Had he *upset* her? He knew darn well she'd wanted him—ached for him to kiss her! But she wouldn't give him the satisfaction! When she turned to face him, she was all-smiles. "Why would I be upset?" she said calmly. "Are you finished for tonight?"

He looked slightly puzzled. "You are upset, aren't you?"

She raised her brows. "That comment about my lips was a compliment, wasn't it? Because I took it as such. And I'm not upset in the least. I'm flattered. Thank you."

She put the teapot on the counter, wiped her hands and walked over to stand in front of him, stopping only when she was close enough to rub bellies—but didn't. "Perhaps, though, we ought to kiss—really kiss—and release the tension of wondering what it would be like. That way we could get on with work and put a stop to all those niggling, runaway thoughts.''

His eyes widened. Before he could do more than part his lips to respond, Mary placed her hands on either side of his jaw and pulled his head toward hers.

It was supposed to be a joke, but she realized too late that the joke was on her. The moment her lips touched his, her heart skipped several beats, then settled into an irregular rhythm that was twice as fast as normal. When Greg's hands circled her waist, her breath caught in her throat. His tongue battled and subdued hers as she touched the back of his neck, glorying in his thick, silky hair, running it through her fingers.

She couldn't believe she was reacting to his kiss this way as if she had a hundred rainbow colors flaring in her head all at once.

Greg tightened his hold on her, pulling her soft body to meet his hardness.

A moan sounded deep in her throat; he echoed it. Wanting to continue, but afraid of where her actions were leading, Mary pulled away. She had to focus on the problem she'd been trying to solve.

She looked up at Greg as if through a haze, then smiled slowly, blinking several times to bring herself back to reality. ''Well, now that that experiment is out of the way, let's get back to work.''

Turning away, she silently promised herself she'd collapse as soon as he left the premises.

But Greg wasn't going to let her off the hook that easily. His arm shot out and captured her. "That wasn't an experiment, Mary. That was a dare." His voice was a deep, rich growl that seemed to vibrate down her spine.

"Call it as you see it. I can't stop you."

"At least be woman enough to look me in the eye and tell me you didn't do that for shock value."

Mary looked him in the eye. "I did do it for shock value. That doesn't mean I didn't enjoy it."

He smiled, his skin crinkling at the corners of his hazel eyes. "By damn, I think I met the last honest woman on earth. Even if you did answer under duress."

She smiled.

Greg ran a hand through his hair, confusion clouding his face. "I wish I knew what the hell to do next."

"Go home?" she asked sweetly, her smile still playing about her mouth. She couldn't help it— she was having a great time. Sparring with Greg was almost as invigorating as kissing him. Almost. "Or how about getting my electronic system out of danger?"

"Okay." His gaze was as heated as a furnace. "But if I demand payment of a kiss occasionally, remember that you set the precedent."

"I'll remember no such thing," she retorted. She turned toward the old fuse box in the corner of the kitchen and opened it wide. "One kiss is one kiss. That's all it is. It's not a promise of more."

"I forgot, women's lib is alive and well," he muttered with a sigh. But there was still an intense gleam in his eye.

"If that means that women are equal to men, you're darn right." When she turned to confront him, he was looking smug. He'd obviously expected to raise her hackles with that comment.

Her gaze narrowed. "Was this a setup?"

"Yup."

And she'd played right into his hands. "Why?"

"Because I know how hard it is to be a female in business. I watched it happen all the time to my wife." He hesitated, then corrected himself, "My ex-wife. You need to be tough if you're going to get ahead. I just wanted to know if you could handle it."

Hands on her hips, Mary Ellen faced him, her anger carefully in check. "If you're testing me, then you can stop right now. You offered me a job and I accepted. We exchanged contracts and money. I'm hired. I don't need to be tested by you or anyone else."

"You're right and I'm sorry. I apologize."

She hadn't expected his apology so quickly. He even *looked* repentant. But she pressed on anyway. "You wouldn't have done this to a man."

"You're right. I'm ashamed."

She saw the glimmer in his eye. "Well…" She turned away, unwilling to let him see the smile she was trying so hard to quell. She had to hand it to him. She'd gotten up a head of steam and he'd diffused it effortlessly.

A few minutes later, Greg was going from room to room inspecting the wiring and taking notes, as if there was nothing on his mind besides electricity. He ended up in the attic, with Mary Ellen right behind him. Even she could see what bad shape things were in; the wires were like brittle rope.

She followed Greg down the stairs and into her office, where he sat and scrawled numbers on another piece of paper. Finally, heaving a hefty sigh, he tossed the pencil on her desk and leaned back. His gaze riveted on her, he broke the bad news. "Almost everything needs to be replaced, Mary. Your wiring is outdated, and in some cases downright dangerous."

She perched on the edge of her desk, her heart dropping at the thought of what all this was going to cost. "I was afraid of that. What did you find?"

"It looks like some areas of the house were re-wired about twenty years ago. The upstairs and downstairs baths have newer wiring. And half the kitchen." He shook his head. "Don't ask me why only half a kitchen, but that's the way it is." He glanced down at his notes again. "And—just by luck—the studio has some decent wiring in it.

At least it's good enough to continue to use for a while."

"It's terrible, isn't it?" she asked, already feeling defeated. Although she'd received his first check, there wouldn't be nearly enough money left over to get the whole thing done.

"Pretty bad," he agreed calmly. "But then, you knew that."

She saw dollar signs flying through the roof. Every dime she had and more was tied up in this house and business, and there was no other way out except to sell it now and take a loss.

"I'll need about three hundred dollars for supplies to begin with. Then, in the next week or so, I'll need more."

Her breath came out in a whoosh. "Three hundred dollars?"

He nodded.

"That's all?"

He grinned. "Lucky for you, you've got a top-notch electrical engineer who gets a discount for parts and knows how to work cheaply. And will."

Her laughter was her answer. "Lucky for me."

"I'll start on the downstairs first."

"Oh, of course," she said, reaching in the side drawer and pulling out her checkbook. She scribbled the amount as if he would change his mind if she didn't write it immediately. When she was finished, she tore off the check and handed it to him.

Greg slipped it into his pocket. "Will you be here tomorrow night?"

Her brows rose. "Of course."

"Don't you ever go out?"

She looked surprised. "You mean for a night shoot?"

"No. I mean as in 'go out'—meet friends, dine, dance, have a good time."

She felt hers cheeks heat. "Of course I do."

His gaze probed. "With anyone in particular?"

"Not in the romantic sense."

"Good."

Her chin tilted stubbornly. "Don't think it means anything. I'm just in a working mode right now. I don't have time to worry about a relationship." She gazed out the window, unwilling to look him in the eye.

Silence hung heavily in the air and she knew Greg was waiting her out. Well, she could play along.... "How long do you think it will take?" she asked. She wanted to know when the job would be completed and, against all good sense and reason, she wanted to know when she'd see him again.

"At least a month or so. Remember, I still have a day job," he teased, going along with the change of subject. But Mary Ellen had a feeling he hadn't forgotten their previous exchange.

"I thought that was a piece-of-cake kinda work. Not fun and challenging like this will be."

He gave a husky chuckle. "You may be right. But it puts food on the table and money into my old age savings. If this job doesn't finish me off first."

"That rough?"

"That rough." He grinned. "But I think I can handle it."

Mary Ellen stood, unwilling to look as if she was holding him there against his will. Or worse, stalling for time. "In that case, I'll see you when I see you."

"Tomorrow night. I'll bring dinner."

"Again?"

"Why not? I have to eat somewhere and it might as well be close to my night job."

"I take mustard on my hamburger."

"I'll bring something a little more substantial," Greg told her. "Hamburgers are my specialty, but I can get pretty sick of them. Not even Jason can eat them every night. And if he's not there, I hardly ever eat at home."

She wasn't going to offer to get all domestic and cook for him. After all, she wasn't her sister Virginia, who loved it. Or her sister Elizabeth, who could whip up twelve meals in under fifteen minutes. For Mary, food was a means to keep alive. At a later date, well, maybe... She gave a delicate shrug. "Fine."

Greg cocked his head and stared down at her. The laugh lines around his mouth and eyes eased as he became more serious. "Tell me, Mary Ellen Gallagher. What is it about me that makes you so wary? Do I offend you in some way? Do I part my hair on the wrong side of my head? Have I said something that turns you off? Do you hate my cologne?"

"Of course not," she protested weakly. "I don't have anything against you." She turned and led the way to the door. "I just don't think it's a good idea to mix business with pleasure."

Greg's brows rose in disbelief. "You mean the business of doing the video for me versus the pleasure of me doing your electrical work?"

"Well, I mean..." She took a deep breath. "Yes."

"I don't believe it."

She confronted him, her chin quivering slightly with the effort, forcing herself to give him a look that was as direct as his. "It's true. You have a life of your own, yet you get to see my private life. And if you get to know me too well, you might have a problem being impartial when you judge my work. I don't want that."

"Do you want me to forget the electrical job here? Will that make you feel better?"

"No. I..." she began, then halted. What was the matter with her? Where else was she going to get an electrician to do all this work for next to nothing? Couldn't she handle a situation like this without becoming frazzled? After all, he was a good-looking man, but still—just a man.

His quick grin caused a sizzling sensation down her spine. Then suddenly he looked surprised. "You're afraid of me, aren't you?"

Mary took a deep breath. "Maybe."

"Why?"

"At the risk of repeating myself, you're still in a relationship with your ex-wife."

Greg looked stunned. Obviously, that wasn't what he'd expected. "You still think you don't want to have anything to do with me because I get along so well with my ex-wife?"

She nodded.

"I don't believe it. I would have thought that it was a big plus in my favor that Janet and I could still be friends even though we're divorced."

"Are you really just friends—and no more?"

"Darlin', if we were more than that, we'd still be married."

She knew better. "Not necessarily."

"Take my word for it. Janet and I are still good friends, but we're not married—in any sense of the word." He bent forward and gave Mary Ellen a moist kiss that made her want more. Much more. "I'll see you tomorrow night armed with dinner and enough wire to wrap around the outside of this house."

"Okay," she whispered, willing to accept his version of his past marriage. A small bubble of happiness seemed to be forming inside her, for the first time in ages, and all she wanted to do was enjoy the feeling.

Greg opened the door, then stopped and glanced over his shoulder. "See you tomorrow night."

Then he was gone.

Mary locked the doors and turned off the lights before making her way up to her bedroom.

As she began stripping off her clothes she suddenly realized how tired she was.

Tossing back the sheets, she climbed into bed and hoped she wouldn't dream of the man. He was just a client and worker, she told herself. He was also the sexiest man she'd ever met. But what drew her even more was his sensitivity. He had an uncanny ability to read her emotions.

She had to remind herself to enjoy what they had now—a friendly, playful flirtation—because it could never go any further. She wasn't about to screw up an account worth thousands for a relationship with no future beyond a roll in the hay.

But she looked forward to having fun with him for the moment....

AFTER WORKING in a pasture filming cows all day, Mary Ellen showered and changed into long pants and a long-sleeved shirt, which warmed her sore muscles. She hurt from lugging equipment and holding weird positions in a field filled with more potholes, stickers and ants than cattle. It wasn't easy to make the cattle look contented and the scene serene, but she thought she'd succeeded. Editing the film tomorrow morning would tell the tale.

Greg was on time and she was ready for him.

"I'll put the tea on the table while you unpack those goodies," she said, moving toward the counter where a pitcher, glasses and ice cubes in a bucket were lined up for use.

"You're in a hurry," Greg commented as he put down the bags. "Have you got a late date?"

She gave him a look that told him how silly he was. "I'm one hungry woman—starving, in fact."

"Pretend we have all the time in the world."

Mary gave a resigned sigh. Men always had to stage their efforts, she thought heartlessly. But there was no compromise; the man had bought it and brought it. If she wanted to dine in companionable peace, she might as well do as he requested.

Mary sat across from where Greg stood and crossed her hands on the table, gazing up at him with fluttering eyelashes and an insipid smile. As if to emphasize the pointlessness of his request, her stomach gave a loud growl.

His eyes widened. "You mean what you say, don't you?"

She smiled smugly. "I told you so."

"And you love being right."

Her grin widened. "More than you know."

Greg tossed the napkins on the table and reached for the packages of condiments in the bag. "I give up. Dig in and help me unload this stuff. Just don't taste anything until both of us can eat."

"Yes, sir!" Mary reached for the other bag, pulling out one container after another. The smell was tantalizing, the packaged heat inviting. After emptying one bag, she grabbed two plates and forks and sat back down. She wouldn't comment on the fact that it was almost the same meal they'd had last night. "I do love Chinese."

"This is Thai. How do you feel about hot stuff?" Greg asked, opening several containers.

Mary didn't miss a beat. "This could be possum belly and I'd eat it."

She downed her soup, then got to work sampling from every one of the twelve containers. The food was delicious—similar to Chinese, yet slightly different in taste and texture. And spicy.

"That was excellent, chef," Mary Ellen exclaimed at last, leaning back in her chair, completely stuffed. "You were right. Spicy." She wiped her forehead daintily.

"Lady," Greg said in admiration, "you sure can pack the food away. Why aren't you as big as a house?"

"It's in my genes," she stated modestly. "My whole family is thin. Except our mother. She was plump when she died. I have a feeling that I'll balloon with age, but if Mother is any indication, that won't be until I'm in my late sixties."

"If then. We didn't know exercise helped the body as well as the mind when your mother was entering retirement age."

"True," she said with a sigh. "And now it's time to pack the containers away. I've got lots of work to do before sunrise."

"Yes, ma'am. So do I."

It took no time at all to clean up and get the kitchen ready for the morning. They worked together as if they'd been doing it all their lives. *Careful, girl,* she told herself. *Teamwork does not a relationship make.* Although she knew that, she couldn't help feeling good about their ability to predict each other's actions. And the sense of sharing fed her soul. She'd never had a man share kitchen duty before. Or any other duty, for that matter. It was a wonderful feeling.

Greg reached for the toolbox Mary had placed on the counter earlier and began sorting through it. She pretended not to notice just how good he looked in a pair of warm-up pants and a black sweatshirt. His clothes weren't new or designer styled; they looked worn and comfortable. And they clung nicely to his muscular butt and shoulders.

"You work out." The words slipped from her mouth before she could stop them.

Greg continued to rummage in the tool kit. "Yes, I do. And you."

"I used to. Not anymore. My job keeps me fit."

"Same thing. You still look great."

"Thank you."

He looked over his shoulder, his gaze taking in every inch of her. "And does your job allow any time just for you?"

She gave a shrug. "Occasionally."

"And for anyone else? Someone new in your life?"

She looked at him warily. "If I decide so. Yes."

Greg finally turned around. "Good. Then please decide to have dinner with me Friday night. I made reservations at one of my favorite places, hoping to enjoy your company."

"I can't."

"You can. You choose not to." His correction was right on target. They both knew it.

"Greg, I..." she began, then floundered for words to explain her fears.

"It's too late," he stated quietly. "I'm not going to back down unless you've absolutely got your mind made up that I'm not interesting enough for you to spend a few hours with. Or unless you have something really important to do that evening, like washing your hair or looking at old movies that make you cry or gardening at midnight. Or unless you're sick...."

She had to laugh. He was knocking down every argument she could possibly think of. Except one.

"Or unless you think you could never be attracted to someone like me, who's so involved with the wonders of magnetic pumps and how they work...."

"Quite the contrary," she finally admitted.

"Does that mean there's hope?"

"There's a problem. I don't want to get involved with someone who might someday discover that he's still interested in his first love. It's already happened to me once. I won't let it happen again. Friday night is definitely out."

"Poor Mary Ellen." His voice was soft, tender, and held just a hint of laughter. "Burned once and doesn't want to start a pattern."

She felt that long-ago hurt flare up as if it had happened yesterday instead of three years ago. "You bet. And from what I can see, you show every sign of putting me through that type of hell." She left off the word *again*. It wasn't necessary; it hung in the air.

He came nearer, his mere closeness taking her breath away. "I have every intention of putting you through something, Mary Ellen, but it sure as hell won't be the mess of a bad love affair, unless you make it so."

"Don't tell me it's all *my* fault if something goes wrong," she began, her voice higher than she wanted. "I'm not the one at fault here."

"Why blame anyone? We haven't done anything...yet." He bent his head to within inches of hers. "But I won't swear to what might happen just minutes from now." His voice was husky and low, evoking sensations that trickled down her spine and curled around her stomach.

She couldn't resist the overwhelming urge to taste his mouth, and reached up to rest her hands on his shoulders. She felt dreamy, soft, pliable....

"You want this to happen just as much as I do," he murmured, his eyes half-closed in anticipation of their kiss.

Some small part of her fought through the haze. "Do not," she answered, but it sounded more like a plea that should have ended with the word *stop*.

As if he'd heard that, too, he fiercely claimed her mouth. Mary held on to his shoulders as the heat of his kiss spread through every part of her body.

His hands were pulling at her waist, then they slipped to her hips and drew her closer still, holding her in a gentle vise against his hard body.

Ever so slowly and with a will of their own, her arms encircled his neck. She felt the ridged muscles across his back and neck and marveled at the leashed power, the brute strength.

She couldn't deny it for one more second—she yearned for, *needed* the contact of his body with hers. It had been too long since someone had made her feel wanted and cherished in a purely feminine way....

Greg's hand edged up over her stomach lavishly caressing her slim body before finally settling on her breast. He flicked her nipple with his thumb, and she arched into his hand. She wanted more, she wanted him to...

He pulled away from her mouth and buried his head in the crook of her neck, his lips still hot and moist from their kiss. A low groan echoed from deep inside him. She knew the same feeling of wonder that he must have felt. Her breath was light and shallow as she tilted her head back to allow him better access.

She prayed Greg would take her right there on the kitchen table. On the floor. She didn't care. She just knew she wanted him more than she'd wanted anything. Ever. The aching need to complete this union with him was so strong it over-

rode everything—every ounce of levelheaded-
ness she'd ever known. Consequences be
damned. She'd never felt this way before and
truly believed, on a gut level, that she'd never
feel this way again.

Greg's mouth returned to claim hers and she
pressed herself against him. She gave a kittenlike
moan, telling him in any language that she
needed him to fill her. She needed him to take the
lead and complete this dance of love....

Greg pulled away, resting his forehead on her
shoulder, catching his breath. Mary's hands
danced across his broad shoulders and arms. She
still wanted more.

"Damn," he whispered raggedly. "I wasn't
prepared for this. If I had been, we wouldn't be
standing here in the kitchen."

"Where would we be?" she asked, goading
him into admissions she needed to hear, if only
for her ego's sake.

"In your bedroom. On your bed. Making
love."

Her stomach clenched at the image. "And
what's stopping us?"

"Protection."

Of course. Where was her head? She was
thankful to him for remembering, even as she
wished he hadn't.

"Unless...?"

She shook her head slowly. "No, I don't," she
said, answering his unspoken question. She'd always left that part of lovemaking up to Joe....

"Well, have no fear, Mary." Greg soothed her hair, then stroked her cheek as he gave a resigned sigh. "The right time will come. And when it does, neither one of us will have reason to regret or worry." He gave a low growl. "Well, at least tonight we won't worry. But I *know* I'll regret this!"

Now that he'd stopped kissing her, Mary Ellen managed to find enough of her voice, and her self-respect, to answer. "There won't be another time."

The corners of Greg's hazel eyes crinkled in laughter. "Don't believe that for a minute, my lady. We'll have this opportunity again, and when we do, it'll be like the fourth of July."

"Braggart. I'm not impressed."

He kissed the tip of her nose, with a knowing look that belied her comment. "But for right now, I'm going home to sit in a tub of ice cubes. I'll be back tomorrow night with the rest of the wire. We'll work first, then we'll play."

He turned to leave, but she called to him, "I won't be here."

"Yes, you will." His voice was calm. Confident. "I'll see you."

She stood in the kitchen and watched him stride to the front door. His walk was one of confidence and manliness. Could it be that *everything* he did exuded total male sexuality?

5

GREG UNLOCKED THE DOOR to his penthouse apartment and strode directly to the bar. He carefully poured himself a short Scotch and then walked to the glass wall that overlooked the Galleria area and downtown. Janet's condominium was two floors below, on the opposite side of the building. She overlooked the Astrodome and the verdant Hermann Park, which rolled out in front of her. Janet liked the trees and the peaceful terrain.

Not Greg. He liked the flash and lights of an active downtown. The skyline was spectacular at night. He had all the most brilliant lights and award-winning architecture of the third largest city in the United States was just outside his window, highlighted against the night sky. When he was younger, he'd yearned for a view like this.

Not tonight, though. Tonight Greg saw none of it.

Instead, his gaze was focused inward, seeing in his mind's eye the run-down little 1920s house with great potential in the Heights, and the woman who lived there. A woman who buried her happiness and inner joy so deep that it made him want to mine it out of her, one shining diamond after another.

There was no doubt in his mind that Mary Ellen Gallagher was a gem. The more he knew of her, the more he saw of her work, the more he realized what a multifaceted, vulnerable and forthright woman she was—and the more he wanted to know better.

Taking a sip of his drink, he stared out at the view he'd paid so much for, and admitted the one big truth that had claimed his thoughts tonight. From that very first moment when he'd seen her in her kitchen, shorts and jogging bra worn like armor, he'd wanted to bed her. He'd wanted to make love to her until she cried for mercy. He wanted to be the greatest lover she'd ever had, showing her just how wonderful and powerful and masculine he could be. He'd wished he were Neanderthal Man so he could drag her back to his cave and hold her captive until she begged for him to never leave her, never stop holding her, never stop making love to her.

There. The nasty reality was out in the open. He'd known it all along, but he had tried to hide his upended emotions, pretending he wanted to be a friend, a business associate, a good-time buddy.

Bull.

He wanted to be her full-time lover.

Another thought rolled in on top of that one. Although he hadn't been completely celibate since the breakup, those churning sexual feelings and strong desires were a first since his divorce. Before he met Mary, he'd wanted to prove his manhood. Now he wanted to ease the ache she created in him. The ache that Mary caused all by herself, not just the ache of losing Janet.

When Janet decided that their marriage was over, he'd told himself it was only a blow to his pride. And he'd believed that. But as the reality of the divorce hit him and the loneliness of his new life set in, he realized just how much he'd taken Janet for granted in a thousand different ways. She'd been his best friend since he was a kid; she'd been his organizer, and above all a buffer between him and the rest of the world. And all the time he'd been buried in his business, he'd naively thought that he was helping physically, contributing emotionally to their household, and sharing the care of their nine-year-old son. That was a laugh!

If he'd changed at all directly after the breakup, it was to develop an ever sharpening awareness of how he hadn't a clue about relating to those who weren't in business with him.

After the divorce, their joint friends had gravitated toward Janet, where they received the attention and care friends needed. Greg hadn't known how to befriend someone or chat about nothing or just enjoy the silent presence of another. And in the years they'd been together, he hadn't taken advantage of learning those lessons from his wife.

Since the breakup Greg had been overwhelmed with invitations to charity dinners and luncheons. He hadn't known one charity from the other—which ones were important, which were spending more money on administration than on the cause itself.

Women, far more forward than he remembered from college, had come on like gangbusters. He wasn't sure whether it was because he was wealthy, good-looking, witty or just plain single. When he glanced in the mirror, he saw a nice-looking man, but nothing to go gaga over. He hadn't known who to trust.

More lessons.

His son was the only person he was relaxed with; there was no posturing, no worrying about manners, nothing. Jason had been agreeable to living one month with his mom, one month with his dad. But the first month Greg had Jason all to himself, he'd gone crazy. He hadn't known what snacks to buy, how much time it took to complete homework assignments, how to balance everything so he'd be home on time for dinner. He wasn't sure how to talk about subjects he'd usually left to Janet. Most of all, he'd had no idea how much energy and time a child consumed. It had dawned on Greg that he'd definitely handled the light side of the load when it came to child rearing. He was *still* learning.

When he'd been a kid growing up with an alcoholic, single dad, Greg had prayed for someone to love him. As a young teenager, he'd searched for someone to love. But when he'd finally found Janet, he'd treated her as if she was his due. For all those years he'd prayed and God had given him Janet. Then he'd lost her through his own stupid neglect. Now the dearest person in his life was his son. Jason was the sun, moon and stars to him. But Greg needed and wanted a female life companion.

He had been really surprised that Janet didn't hate him for all his neglect and absences. Instead, she'd been gracious and more than helpful, guiding him into activities and social groups, giving lots of information regarding Jason. Thank goodness it had been an amicable breakup. Again, thanks to Janet. She'd taught Greg to stop pouting, pointing out how much easier it would be on Jason—who was their main responsibility. Jason wasn't the cause of the divorce, she'd told Greg, and shouldn't be the recipient of any stress over it. It took a little growing up on his part, but Greg had finally agreed. Now he was glad he had.

One more giant step....

Tonight, when Mary Ellen had accused him of still being in love with Janet, he had immediately scoffed at the idea. But it wasn't that far-fetched. For a while after their separation, he'd been convinced that if he could win her back everything would be the same. Things would go back to being the way they used to be. It took a long time for him to realize that the way things were was what had made Janet leave in the first place.

He'd loved her, admired her mind as well as

her body, brought her in as his business partner, worked with her every day, got her pregnant and made a mother out of her. Then he'd done the most stupid thing he'd ever done in his life. He'd forgotten that the main reason they were together was because he loved her and she loved him and they wanted to be with each other. That's what being in love was supposed to mean.

Love—such a small word for such an enormous event in one's lifetime. Until he'd lost love he hadn't realized just how precious a flower it was.

He discovered that, just like a garden, the more that emotion was fed, watered and tended, the better it bloomed. But let love fend for itself and, sooner or later, it died, leaving weedy memories and thorny regrets.

Greg gulped down the rest of his drink. Although he loved Jason with every fiber of his being, that wasn't enough. He needed a mate. He didn't know if Mary was "the one," but for right now the look he saw in her eyes made him feel good about himself.

Feeling like a wolf who'd just spied a plump white rabbit, Greg smiled, and promised himself that Mary Ellen Gallagher would give him a chance to be with her.

MARY HAD FELT NERVOUS all day.

Greg had said he'd be back tonight, and she expected him any minute. She'd actually made a tuna-broccoli salad for dinner—just in case he hadn't eaten. While the broccoli cooked, she busied herself by emptying the contents of one long string of cabinets into boxes and piling them on the side wall. She'd decided to paint the interior of the cabinets, and she was starting with the longest section.

Where was he?

She put a paper plate between two glass ones and placed them in an empty box.

He was supposed to be here right after work.

She grabbed two more plates.

He'd said he'd do the electrical renovations, and she'd given him a check for supplies. So far he hadn't done a thing except drop off some wire. Was he fleecing her?

She reached for a glass and put a paper cup over it, then stacked another glass outside it.

That was silly. The man was a millionaire, for heaven's sake! He was probably too busy to spend spare time fooling around with an old house and a woman who wouldn't give him more than the time of day.

But he had promised to help, dammit! If he wasn't going to do the job, he shouldn't have volunteered and gotten her hopes up and her dreams churning again. Of course, those dreams were about the house, not the man....

There was a loud knock on the kitchen door and Mary Ellen jumped, dropping a glass to the floor. Turning, she saw Greg through the window, and couldn't quite stop the smile that lit up her face.

"Happy to see me?" he asked when she opened the door. His face was ruddy from the stiff, chilly breeze, and he held a box in his hands.

"Relieved. I thought you were a ghost."

"Liar," he said, placing the box on the table and turning to take her in his strong arms and plant a hello kiss on her parted lips. His kiss was returned in force. She was unprepared to deflect him—or at least that's what she told herself.

His mouth was cool and firm and felt so very *right*. When he pulled away, he smiled in his sexy way. "And a very good evening to you, too."

"You're filled with spit and vinegar tonight," she commented, trying not to let on how upsetting his kiss really was. She was glad he wasn't touching her, or he might have felt her quickened heartbeat, her shallow breath, her erratic pulse. Her confused state....

"I'm just a guy who enjoys kissing you," he said, ignoring the undercurrents and digging into the supplies he'd brought tonight. "Tomorrow I need to be here first thing in the morning before you begin your workday."

"Why?"

"Because I have to turn off the electricity, and I think you'd rather I do that when you're least in need."

That made sense. And, strangely, it made her heart beat even faster. "For how long?"

"An hour or so."

A mental list of all the things she needed to do

tomorrow rose to mind. "Couldn't you do it at night?"

"And work by flashlight?" he asked dryly.

She grinned sheepishly. "I'll hold it for you. Only joking!" she exclaimed before he could answer. "Of course you can do it in the morning. I wasn't thinking."

"You wouldn't want to put me up for the night, would you?" His voice was casual, the question thrown out between them as if she was asked that every night of the week.

The *real* question registered and a resounding *no!* rang in her head. But her mouth wouldn't obey her brain. "Why do you ask?"

"Because if I could get to it around six-thirty, I'd probably be through with the fuse box wiring an hour before my first meeting."

"The guest room has a bed in it, but it's not cleaned up for company," she said slowly, mulling over and discarding the other, most obvious alternative.

His hazel eyes twinkled. "That's okay. I'm not company, I'm your friendly neighborhood electrician, remember?"

"Of course, my *millionaire* electrician," she said dryly. "The one who doesn't mind sleeping in a room that's being used for storage."

"Don't go all uptight on me, Mary. If your Irish upbringing can't handle the thought, I'll go home tonight and come back in the morning. It's no big deal."

But it was a big deal, and Mary Ellen couldn't

let it alone. Even as she poured paint into a pan, she was ribbing him. "You want to spend the night and it's no big deal?"

"That's right." He stripped rubber from the end of a loop of wire.

Stirring the paint, her heart pounding like a huge hammer, she shrugged and said, "Okay by me."

Greg stopped, looked up. "You're sure?"

Mary Ellen hopped up to perch on the counter, then took her paintbrush and pretended to study the cabinet. She felt his heated gaze but ignored it. "Sure. After all, we're not talking about an affair, just a sleeping arrangement."

"And that thought doesn't bother you?"

Mary gave a short laugh. "Why? Are you a rapist? A killer? Did you beat your wife and are you looking for someone else to bat around?"

"None of the above. But how would you know for sure?"

"Because you like your work and you want to keep doing it. No one in his right mind would deliberately ruin his life with the other stuff," she said, taking the first brush stroke. "Besides, your wife still likes you. If you'd had any tendencies in that vein, you'd have shown them by now and she wouldn't have anything to do with you."

"Not even for money? Lots of money?"

"She would have sued you for every dime you have and held you up to public ridicule. And she certainly wouldn't be sharing custody of her only child with you."

"Gee, thanks," Greg stated dryly. "It's nice to know that my reputation is based on my ex-wife's reactions."

Mary Ellen's laughter bubbled up. "Would you give me that glass of iced tea next to the stove please?"

"Of course," he murmured, handing it to her. "And for your birthday, I'll give you a share of stock in the company. I think you'll single-handedly keeping it going with sales from your video."

"When you're right, you're right." She grinned before downing half the glass.

The low tunes of seventies rock filtered from the office to the kitchen as they worked together in an easy silence. Greg wired the countertop for two new outlets that would be active later, when the main wiring was complete. They stopped for a break and Mary served the tuna salad. Within half an hour, they were back at work.

Occasionally Greg would hum along with the music. Occasionally Mary would sing a bar or two of a song. Then they'd laugh and keep working.

It was the most relaxing yet entertaining evening Mary had ever spent with a man.

He was sexy, warm, funny and totally at ease and natural. And he was endearing himself to Mary's heart. It wasn't fair. This man wanted a fling, not a wife. Not that she wanted to be a wife right now. She dreamed of having freedom to pursue her career. Even so, this was all wrong. So why did it feel so very right?

When they were finally done for the night, it was past eleven. Mary's arms hurt from the un-usual positions painting the cabinets had de-manded. And the old black insides looked more like gray than the nice bright white she had en-visioned.

As if reading her mind, Greg commented, "Disheartening, isn't it?"

"I hope it looks better with a second coat."

"Three coats will do it," he predicted, giving a stretch that showed off his muscular chest and arms. Very nice indeed. Mary Ellen wondered if he'd done that on purpose. "Show me where to bed down. I think I'm ready for a good night's rest."

"Sure," she said, putting the brush in a jar of mineral spirits to soak and sealing up the paint while Greg checked the downstairs doors.

Mary led the way upstairs. A dim lamp at the end of the hallway provided barely enough light to see the railing. "Hall light doesn't work, so please watch your step."

"I'll look at it next time," Greg promised, his husky voice confirming just how close to her he was.

"Your bedroom is to the left," she said, her voice sounding a little shaky. "Bathroom's to the right." She turned to the right as Greg headed to-ward the left. "I'll meet you there. I need to get some linens for you."

"Okay," he called over his shoulder, opening the only door in that hallway and stepping in.

Mary's heart tripped in her breast as she quickly gathered an extra blanket and sheets. When she was through, she went into her own room and grabbed two of the many pillows off her bed and brought them with her.

She reached the door, stopped still and stared at the man who was staring out the window. He stood at an angle and had such a sad look on his face that it touched her somewhere deep inside and set off her own emotions. She wanted to cry; she wanted to give him a hug. She wanted to make love to him.

Just then he turned and gazed at her. There was no shield between them, no hidden meanings or covert looks or guessing. They were two people who desperately needed each other for comfort and love.

Still silent, he reached out to her, asking her to be with him.

In silence she answered, shaking her head. It was a reluctant no at best, but a no just the same.

She couldn't take a chance on losing her focus now. She was so close to success. Why had he come into her life now, when she was most determined not to have a man muddle up her plans? She needed all the energy she had to achieve her goals. It just wouldn't work.

He smiled, looking just as sad as he had earlier. "Do I get a kiss good-night?"

"Will it end there?"

"I'll follow your lead."

Even after her silent denial, temptation was too mighty. And she could stop after one kiss....

Mary dropped the sheets and pillows on the bed and bravely walked to his side. His smile was so endearing that, without even realizing it, Mary's hand cupped his jaw and cheek. "You're certainly unusual, Mr. Torrance," she said huskily.

His hand covered hers, holding her palm against the light sandpaper of his beard. "I'd use the same word to describe you, Ms. Gallagher."

He dragged her hand across his firm lips, and when she felt the heat of his tongue scorch the very center of her palm, she jerked. He kept a tight grip on her, however. "Don't be frightened. I just needed to taste you."

"Do I taste like paint?" she asked, her voice almost a whisper.

"You taste like a field of clover warmed in sunshine."

"Liar."

"And ambrosia," he added, his thumb touching the center of her bottom lip. With his thumbnail, he traced the outside of her parted lips, then touched her front teeth, slipping his thumb into her mouth.

Instinctively, she gave a gentle suck.

His hazel eyes gleamed and breath hissed between his gritted teeth. "Don't stop."

Before she could react, his mouth replaced his thumb and his kiss deepened, sending undulating heat waves through her body. Her legs felt weak, and she wrapped her arms around him. Her world rocked; her head reeled. Somewhere in the great vast distance, she was sure she heard bells—deep resonant bells that pealed with joyous abandon.

His hands pressed her hips to his and she felt every indentation, every protrusion against her own soft femininity. His body swayed back and forth against hers, and she helped, easing the ache that flamed quickly into need. That wondrous feeling settled in her abdomen, heating, quickening, itching to be assuaged.

When his mouth left hers, her lips felt chilled until he pressed her head against his shoulder and buried his face in the curve of her neck. With astonishment, she realized that he was shaking.

He kissed the curl of her ear. "You pack a punch."

"So do you."

"I want to make love to you, Mary Ellen." He pulled back and looked down at her. Her hair was tousled, her lips swollen and damp from his kiss. "Will you let me? Will you come to bed with me?"

"Yes," she whispered, mesmerized by his moving lips. They were such beautiful lips....

"With no worries in the middle of the night or regrets in the morning?"

"Yes." Her eyes widened. "No!"

His brows rose. "So the lady has come to her senses."

"Yes." She pulled away, but only as far as his arms would allow. "You got your kiss good-night, Greg. Let's not get greedy."

"And ruin a great friendship?" His tone was dry, crisp.

"That's right." She stared at his chest, willing her heartbeat to slow before she looked up beseeching. "We're getting into dangerous territory here. Let's not do something we'll both regret."

"Speak for yourself, Mary. I'm not the one running away from something that seems pretty damn special to me. You are. And I'm not even sure if you know why you're doing it."

Mary Ellen gave a sigh. "Neither do I. But I know I'm not ready for this."

"Will you ever be?"

"I don't know. I thought you said we could take this one step at a time," she said, hoping to put off the inevitable and not understanding why. Her mind wouldn't function while her heart raced so quickly.

"We just did," he said patiently. "You are the one who wants to stop here instead of taking that next step." He brushed a lock of jet black hair back from her ear. "But I didn't get where I am by being impatient. We'll slow down." His gaze hardened. "But make no mistake, Mary. Our relationship is heading straight for the edge of that cliff. And when we get there, you'll either have to jump off or trust in me." With great reluctance, he loosened his arms from around her hips. "For both our sakes I hope it's the latter."

Mary didn't answer. She couldn't. What do you say to someone who's already said it all?

6

MARY HEARD A FAINT beep, beep, beep around five o'clock in the morning and recognized the sound as the alarm on Greg's wristwatch. She knew the time because she'd looked at the luminous dial on her own clock just seconds ago. In fact, she'd been glancing at it all night long.

She slipped out of bed and into her robe. If Greg was going to get up at this hour, the least she could do was fix a pot of coffee. Besides, she didn't want him to know just how cranky she could be in the morning before coffee when she didn't get enough sleep. She didn't want him to know just how much his kiss had unsettled her, or that she'd only had an hour's sleep at most between bouts of alertness. She'd heard every squeak and groan of the old timber, thinking it was Greg walking down the hall to her room, coming to claim what she had offered for a moment before sanity reigned once more....

GREG PRESSED THE BUTTON that turned off his watch alarm, placed his hands behind his head and stared at the ceiling with a frown. It was still pitch-black outside. Only a dim streetlamp gave enough light to see the pile of boxes around the perimeter of the room. They were all labeled and neatly stacked.

What a fool he'd been last night!

He'd rushed Mary, trying to get what he wanted without patiently traveling down the road that would get him there—one step at a time. He knew better than that. He needed to slow down, wait till she trusted him.

Greg had to grin. This was almost the turn of the century and he and Mary were acting like throwbacks to the fifties. He doubted most modern couples suffered this kind of angst over to bed or not to bed.

But he *was* trustworthy, he told himself. At least he'd always thought he was, until last night. Last night he'd lost all sense of decorum and gone into urgency mode.

Worse than that, he was beginning to believe in love at first sight. All his life he'd listened to stories of people who'd heard a voice or caught a whiff of a scent and fallen in love—but he'd always been sure it was plain old lust. Now he was acting like those he'd scoffed. He'd seen Mary's smile and fallen in love. He'd never wanted anything more than he wanted to have her in his arms.

He needed to get out of here and gain some perspective—although he was pretty sure leaving wasn't going to matter one iota. He'd return tonight and try to talk her into letting him stay here again.

Although he knew these feelings were more

than lust, he didn't want to examine how much more. But he vaguely recognized the symptoms for what they were. He wanted to know more about her. He wanted to do more than touch her body—he wanted to touch her emotions, too.

He heard soft footfalls on the stairs, moving into the kitchen. Within minutes he smelled coffee brewing.

He smiled. At least she wasn't angry enough to kick him out and threaten never to see him again.

He still had a chance....

WHEN GREG LEFT later that morning, Mary Ellen missed his presence in her house. She felt lonely. That wasn't a good sign. She wanted to be with him. That thought alone rang every danger bell she'd ever heard.

It would pass, Mary told herself all day long. When she repeated her thoughts out loud later that afternoon, Edie disagreed.

"Not until you indulge yourself a little," her friend stated evenly.

"That kind of indulging is dangerous."

"So, be careful," Edie instructed. "But if you don't take a chance once in a while, you'll never stretch. This man could make you...stretch." She grinned wider than a Cheshire cat.

"You're nuts," Mary protested, laughing.

"Of course, but you don't have to involve your heart in this. Just use your head and enjoy."

"Can *you* do that?"

"On occasion," her friend confirmed. "Grant

isn't always lovable, you know. But married people can't just walk away, so sometimes we play a role until we feel good about it again. People come together to feed all sorts of needs. Love is just one of them.'' Edie reached under her desk and pulled out a brown paper bag carefully folded at the top. ''But you see, I'm not sure you know what to do anymore when an opportunity presents itself so handsomely, so I took matters into my own hands and made you a romance package to help you into the next step.''

Mary stared blankly at the bag. ''A what?''

''A romance package,'' Edie repeated patiently. ''It's handy stuff to have around if you're contemplating a night of rip-roaring…fun.''

Carefully, Mary peeled back the folds and looked inside.

''Go ahead, pull it all out.''

She did so, until the bag was empty. Mary's breath whooshed from her lungs. ''Wow, lady. If this is any indication of what your love life is like, I want to see the movie—or make sure Grant is still standing.''

A fat, vanilla-scented candle sat in the center, with at least fifteen small votive candles in all colors piled next to it. There were Hershey's Bars, candy kisses, grapes in a small plastic container, a can of whipped cream and a bottle of wine, two plastic glasses, a massage-for-couples book, a small container of sesame oil, a silk glove and a feather. And a small package of top-of-the-line condoms.

Edie saw her look of shock. "Just have fun with it, Mary. It's not necessary to use it all at once, you know."

"I don't know how to use any of it," Mary Ellen protested, but her mind whirred with images of Greg that demonstrated a long list of possibilities.

"Take one thing, place it where you want it, then go on to the next," Edie said patiently. "Before you know it, you'll come up with a few of your own tricks."

"Really, I…"

"Start with the candles," Edie prompted. "Place the votives on the stairs and lead him up there, keeping the fat one next to your bed."

Mary grinned. "Edie, you're wicked."

"Aren't I though? I love it." Her smile drooped. "Years ago I used to tease Grant this way." Her look was faraway, thoughtful. "Maybe I need to try it again."

Mary gave her friend a piercing look. She'd been so preoccupied with her own problems, she hadn't been paying much attention to Edie's. "Is everything all right between you two?"

Edie forced a smile. "We've just been married too long and need a little surprise put back in our life. Maybe I ought to put together another romance kit for myself."

Mary was prudent enough to keep quiet. If Edie wanted to talk about it, she would say more.

Bundling up her kit, Mary Ellen carried it into

the kitchen, placing it on the table while she made their pot of afternoon tea.

But ideas danced in her head, tantalizing her imagination as much as the thought of Greg coming over tonight did....

BY THE TIME GREG WALKED in the door, looking like a model for casual men's clothing, she was a wreck. He wore a lightweight, hunter green warm-up suit with a pale yellow knit shirt. Even his running shoes looked brand-new, not like her used-to-be-white ones.

He held containers of Post Oak Grill's salad with feta, and bags of hot, crusty bread, and when he opened them, tantalizing scents filled the room.

Mary gazed at the food. She couldn't look him in the eye. Every time she glanced his way, she thought of the romance kit and her quickening senses embarrassed her.

She'd felt so intimidated that she'd purposely worn her faded, paint-splattered bike shorts with what she called her smock—a man's dress shirt tied at her waist and rolled up at the arms. It, too, was colorfully decorated with paint from projects she'd done in the past several years. It was the least sexy thing she had. *That* would show him she wasn't interested!

"Everything all right?" Greg finally asked as they finished eating.

"Everything's fine," she confirmed, focusing great attention on buttering her last bite of bread.

"In that case, can I ask for a repeat of last night?"

Her gaze darted to him, her eyes as wide as a doe's. "What do you mean?"

Greg sighed deeply. "I mean can I spend the night? I have another early meeting and I need to begin rewiring all your sockets in the morning."

"And you already brought your suit and stuff." It was a guess.

He grinned widely, revealing slashes on either side of his mouth. "Yes."

Her heart skipped several beats before settling into a fast-paced rhythm. She gave a shrug and bit into her bread. "Fine."

"Don't get too excited, Mary Ellen. I might think you care."

"I care about *all* my clients."

"Oh, thank you for sharing that." His tone was as dry as hers had been offhand.

Mary quickly finished the meal and cleaned up. She spied Edie's gift on the counter and moved it to the floor by the end cabinets. She'd deal with it another time—when Greg wasn't here.

While she continued painting cabinets, Greg started the tedious job of systematically changing socket wiring in the living room. Her stereo played soft rock, echoing quietly throughout the high-ceilinged house.

Somehow it was both comforting and disturbing to have someone else around the place. For the first two months after Mary had moved in, she had spent each and every evening alone, enjoying the silence of her own thoughts. Until Greg came into her life, she would have sworn that she *preferred* her quiet and solitary nights.

Now all that had changed. How quickly she had adapted to his presence, even agreeing to let him spend the night rather than have him leave.

There was a sense of inevitability about them being together. It was as if she knew this was supposed to happen—just as she knew that they would probably make love. Unless he turned out to be a mass murderer or something equally horrendous, they *would* make love. Oh, not because she would expect him to commit to her. No sirree. That wouldn't happen. She wouldn't become *that* involved again, not with anyone.

No, this time she'd handle it like a man would—she'd play and enjoy and get as close as was necessary for them to have a mutually satisfying time. And then she'd end it.

She thought about mentioning her romance kit to Greg, but couldn't find the words. Heck, she couldn't find the nerve!

She thought about walking up to him, throwing her arms around his broad shoulders and giving him a kiss that removed all doubt about the next move either of them would make. But she couldn't force her legs to carry her in his direction.

So Mary settled for fantasizing about being with him in a loving clinch....

By midnight she was exhausted from taut

nerves, her fevered thoughts and the amount of physical labor the cupboards had required. She felt like a weary, unloved contortionist.

Greg must have felt the same way. He walked into the kitchen, stretching his back, then poured himself a glass of water, downing it in one gulp.

"Got any painkillers?" he asked when he was finished.

"What's the matter?"

"Headache."

Mary found a bottle of aspirin tablets and shook two out into her palm. Greg downed those, too.

"Sit," she ordered.

If he was surprised at her tone, he didn't show it. He took a seat at the kitchen table, resting his arms on the flat surface.

Mary came up behind him, her hands almost shaking with the excitement of touching him. She rested her palms on his shoulders, then began pressing the muscles on both sides of his neck, gradually moving up to his head. Her fingers danced around his temples, then soothed his brow and the bridge of his nose.

"Your hands are magical," he murmured, closing his eyes as she gently followed the curve of his brow.

"Must be all the paint," she teased, her fingers ruffling his scalp. "You, too, could have soft yet pliable hands if you painted more...."

"I'll help tomorrow. I promise," he mumbled.

"As long as you fulfill my dreams by doing this again."

"Well…" She worked around both ears, massaged his earlobes and tugged gently before diving into his hairline again. "Let's see how good you are tomorrow," she teased.

Greg leaned his head back against her, his eyes still closed. "How about let's see how good you are tonight."

It was as if her blush started at her toes, pitched her stomach into a roller-coaster ride, then rose all the way up to the top of her head. "Watch your language, mister. Someone might misunderstand you."

His hazed eyes opened and he stared up at her. "I know what I said."

"Well, how romantic," she murmured dryly, dismissing what felt like a hundred-pound lump in her chest; it was just her heart pounding. "That kind of language should sweep any woman off her feet."

His sleepy, relaxed look of moments before was gone abruptly. Greg turned around, stood up and took her in his arms, his eyes hot with desire. "I want you, Mary Ellen. You're already in my every thought. I want you in my arms and in my bed." His slow, easy grin was endearing. "But I'd settle for having you in *your* bed."

She wanted to be with him in her bed, too. Wasn't this what she'd been thinking of all week long? Hungering for him? His words paved the way, easing her fear of rejection and giving her the strength to be bold. She stood on tiptoe and lightly brushed her mouth against his. "Then why are we standing in the kitchen? Am I supposed to whip you up something first?"

His grin widened. "You're standing in the kitchen because you haven't led me to heaven. Yet."

"And where do you think heaven is?" she asked with a slow, knowing smile.

"Well, darlin', I was going to say your bedroom. But that's wrong." He outlined the curve of her cheek with his palm. "*Anywhere* you are is heaven."

"Don't try flattery now, Greg. It's not necessary," she chided.

"It's the truth."

Her head swam with the need to touch him, feel the strength of him under her hands. "I'd rather be *anywhere* but in the kitchen," she said playfully, feeling braver than she'd ever felt before. "Somehow this paint doesn't smell as good as your aftershave. And a countertop isn't quite as comfortable as a bed."

His eyes crinkled at the corners. "Be adventurous, Mary Ellen. Let's play down here for a few minutes."

Her heart thumped extra hard. "What are you looking for? A chandelier?"

"No. A desk," he said softly, taking the lead and walking slowly down the hall and into the office. "I've always wanted to do this and never have." Mary Ellen's desk had been cleaned of the day's work. The console behind her held a calculator and a telephone.

Greg turned and sat on the edge of the desk, pulling her into the V of his legs. His hungry hazel eyes devoured her. His hands began moving slowly, sensuously, then heated as he reached beneath her shirt to clasp her waist and feel the smooth texture of her skin.

"Your skin is so soft," he whispered, burying his head in the curve of her neck.

She held tightly to his shoulders, her head tilted back so his mouth could reach her throat. It felt fantastic to be touched, to be wanted, to be told such wonderful things. For tonight, at least, she was willing to believe. Tomorrow sanity would return and she would take his intimate, sensual words with large pinches of salt. But not tonight.

His hands rose and cupped her breasts, still encased in her lace bra. His fingers slipped under the front catch and the bra rose up, uncovering her breasts to allow his wandering hands free exploration. She breathed a soft, warm sigh against his temple as he eased the ache in her breast, and then created another one farther down.

Mary slipped her hands inside his shirt, spreading her fingers across his chest and reveling in the feeling of his hair under her palms. She felt the ripple of Greg's muscles as he drew her closer to him. He shivered, and she felt strong and powerful because she was able to generate that response.

"Take off my shirt," he ordered, his voice husky with desire.

With shaking fingers, she did as she was told. When the shirt dropped to the floor, he leaned forward and, with tantalizing slowness, parted the buttons of *her* shirt. When her breasts were bare he stared with unabashed desire. "My God, you're beautiful."

"Look at *all* of me when you say that." She slipped the shirt over her shoulders and let it drop. "Or don't say it at all."

Greg pulled her to him. Then, with tantalizing slowness, he bent his head and allowed his tongue to circle her aureole. With a moan, she held his head against her, praying he would never stop.

When he took her nipple into his warm mouth, she felt dizzy with reaction. Need raced through her body and she arched closer, never wanting to lose contact. Never wanting this to end. "Don't stop," she whispered breathlessly. "Don't... stop."

His laughter was low and throaty. "Don't let me." He teased her other nipple, nudging, tasting, taunting. He began the process of pulling down her shorts as well as her French-cut cotton underpants. When he reached between her thighs, she stiffened. "Don't make me stop, Mary," he almost begged.

At his slow, soft touch, her breath caught in her chest. The feeling was delicious, wondrous.... Her eyes drifted shut, her body swayed to some tantalizing inner music.

"Look at me, Mary Ellen." Greg's voice intruded into her fantasy.

She looked down. His mouth was barely inches away from her breast, his hazel eyes staring up at her, implacable as steel except for an inner light that revealed the heat he was feeling. "Know who I am. Know that it's me with you," he said, and it was more a command than a request.

Her own voice shook as she spoke. "I know you, Greg. I'd know you anywhere."

He smiled. "Then know this, too, my love." He bent his head and covered her mound with his mouth blowing his heated breath softly over her tender flesh.

She heard the moan leave her throat before it echoed in the room. When his tongue darted out to complete the intimate kiss, Mary swooned. She'd never thought she was the swooning type, but now she knew better. She could barely brace her legs as she leaned against the desk to keep her balance, digging her fingers into his shoulders. Her breath sounded raspy. Shallow. Harsh.

When Greg lifted his head, his own rough breathing filled the air. His hands keeping her steady, he stood and wrapped her in his arms. "You are so wonderful, so very responsive. And there's more. So much more." He nibbled on her ear.

But Mary had had enough. Standing naked,

she reached to rid him of his warm-up pants. It was time to take charge.

"You wanted someplace unique, you've got it. Now it's your turn, big boy," she said, not knowing until she tugged his pants down just how accurate that nickname was.

They both smiled.

She cradled Greg gently, pleasuring him as he had pleasured her earlier. With a harsh hiss, he pulled her up onto the desk and entered her. When they were merged together, they both closed their eyes and grew still, reveling in the wondrous feeling of being joined.

When his mouth took hers, she tasted herself there. His tongue conquered hers. His hands roved over her back and breasts, creating more heat wherever he touched. Every thought, every fiber of her being was consumed by the man in her arms, in her heart. Bells rang in her head, warmth radiated through her body and nothing mattered in the whole wide world except Greg.

Liquid excitement filled Mary Ellen's inner vision with pastel-colored rainbows and a golden-yellow sun; wonderful warm feelings floated around her like an aura. And when she exploded, Greg did, too. He arched, then flowed into her, his body growing supple and blending with hers. She held him tightly, hanging on until she could safely float back to earth—and reality.

Greg rested his chin on the top of her head, his breathing still ragged and deep. He held her tightly against him, unwilling or unable to let go just yet. And Mary didn't want to be parted from him, either. She wrapped her arms around his waist, resting her head against the solidness of his chest.

An utter and unbelievable peace invaded her, lapping at the edges of her mind until she was calm and rested, and relaxed about what had just happened.

His deep chuckle reverberated in her ear. "That was fantastic," he murmured with a satisfied sigh. "*You* were fantastic."

"We were fantastic," she said, loving the fact that they could share laughter right now. She liked the fact that, with him, lovemaking wasn't so sacred they couldn't enjoy it. Nor did they have to turn it into something it wasn't—a commitment.

He grinned impishly. "You make me feel like a kid. When can we do it again?"

"Anytime you think you're ready," she teased, feeling wanted and sexy, savvy and so very feminine.

"Now," he stated, kissing the tip of her nose. "Only this time we'll take it slow and easy so I can enjoy every morsel of you."

"It doesn't matter that I'm content now?" she asked, surprised at herself for being so open. She had never said or done half the things she'd said and done this evening.

"Not a whit—unless you don't want to." He gazed down at her with...could it be caring in his eyes? "But this time I want you to tell me what makes you happy."

"Greg, I..." she began. But suddenly she couldn't say what was on her mind. Embarrassment made her cheeks flare with color. How could she make love with a man and then be too embarrassed to discuss any subject? It didn't make sense, but it was happening anyway.

"I know," he said quietly. "Now that you've taken the plunge, you're not quite sure what happens next."

Her eyes gazed at him somberly. "And what does happen next?"

"Does it have to be decided right now? Can't we take this relationship one step at a time?"

She dimpled. "Sounds familiar."

"Doesn't it though? But right now, I want to take you upstairs and hold you all through the night."

"Oh, so you're more tired than you admitted, is that it?" she teased, not knowing what else to say. She had so many questions, but this wasn't the time.

"Not at all, but you are. If you weren't tired you'd be saying all those things on the tip of your tongue."

She felt her face flame again and struggled to formulate a clear sentence. "I was hoping that this wouldn't affect our business relationship."

He cocked a brow. "I thought we'd gone over that when I volunteered to wire the house."

"We did," she said, "but making love isn't the

same as wiring a house. This is much more complicated."

"And yet it's such a simple, elemental act."

"But…"

Greg stood, holding on to her hand. "It's too late to have this discussion. Let's wait for a better time, like after the year 2050. Meanwhile, take me upstairs and have your way with me."

"As in sleep?"

"As in making love slowly, then sleeping." It was a gentle correction, said with a small smile and much warmth in his gaze.

Mary Ellen gave up. She wasn't going to pick apart their evening together tonight. Maybe next week, when he was no longer here, or next month, when she finished with his project. Or even six months from now, when she was alone and wondering why in the world she had purposely done this to herself.

But not now.

She led him up the stairs and down the hall to her bedroom. Suddenly feeling shy, she stood on one side of the bed while he stood on the other and they rolled back the bedspread. Without a word, they slid into bed and into each other's arms.

This time their lovemaking was long and slow and easy. The heat of anxiety was gone, replaced by the comfort of knowing how well they fit together. They stroked and whispered and guided each other. And when she soared to the heavens, Greg gave a deep chuckle, appreciating her climax as much as he enjoyed his own just a few moments later.

Afterward, they lay in each other's arms. Gently, Greg kissed her closed eyelids, gave a contented sigh and fell asleep.

Mary Ellen, on the other hand, stared at the ceiling and wondered how she'd ended up in Greg's arms. With her hand beneath his on his chest, she felt the rise and fall of his even breathing.

Making love had probably been a mistake. Mary was falling out of desire and into love. She said a silent prayer that she was doing the right thing and finally closed her eyes. Edie was right. After coming this far, Mary might as well ride this relationship out and worry about the consequences later.

Who knows? she thought. *There might not be any consequences.*

A hollow voice in the back of her head gave a hearty laugh.

Mary purposely ignored it.

7

THE NEXT EVENING Greg arrived with his arms full of brown grocery bags.

He was dressed casually in another warm-up suit. This one was black and red, with a black T-shirt that hugged his broad chest. His expression was relaxed and easygoing. Just looking at him made her heart happy.

"What's going on?" she asked, following him into the kitchen. All day long she'd silently debated whether or not he'd show up like he'd said he would when he'd left early this morning. Her emotions had gone from high to low to high again. Finally, they'd settled into low as she realized what a fool she'd been to jump into bed with a man she was afraid to admit her love to. What kind of a weak relationship was that? She was becoming too dependent on his presence and his caring, but couldn't turn off her love.

"I've got dinner in one bag and a compact disc player with CDs in another. Nothin' but the best for my gal and me. We're dining and dancing tonight," he announced as he set the bags on the kitchen table. "It's been a hell of a day, and we deserve it."

She loved the way he included her in that assumption. It meant he'd thought of her today, too. Just like the night before, she asked the question she knew would get her in the least amount of trouble. "What's for dinner?"

Instead of telling her, Greg reached out and enclosed her slim waist with his hands, turning her in his arms to face him. His mouth brushed her eyes, her cheeks, her throat. "Kisses and hugs and lots of sweet talk."

"Man cannot live on love alone," she challenged throatily.

He leaned back and looked at her in surprise. "I'd like to test that theory."

She grinned, but it was more to soften her words. "So would every man, until afterward."

"Then what?"

"Then they'd have what they wanted, and they'd disappear like rabbits in a magic show until the next time they got horny."

"Wow," he said softly. "You've really been burned."

"No, but I have friends," she countered, unwilling to discuss her personal mistakes. "We talk. I haven't seen much that would convince me otherwise."

"Don't blame me for what other men have done. Okay?"

Mary Ellen took a deep breath for courage. "That goes both ways, right?"

Greg frowned. "What do you mean?"

"I mean that whatever women have done in your past is exactly that. I'm not those women.

I'm me." She gave a small grin. "Starting now, I'll make my own mistakes with you."

His eyes twinkled with merriment. "Great balls of fire, woman. I finally got you to admit there is an 'us,'" he said, just before kissing her breath away. Her own arms tightened around his shoulders, her head tilting to accommodate him. His lips were firm, warm and such a perfect match to hers.

When he pulled away, she gave a satisfied sigh. "Just for now," she said, as surprised as he was that she had spoken her thoughts aloud.

"I wouldn't dare try to rope you into a relationship that you couldn't control enough to feel safe. That means that you get to call the shots. At least…for now."

"And later?"

"Later, you either learn to trust me or we give up the ghost of the relationship." His gaze was serious as he stared down at her. "I have to be trusted, Mary. It's my requirement for a long-term relationship between us."

She loved the sound of it, but wasn't willing to put any stock in him yet. "And you don't think it's mine?"

"I don't know. You haven't spoken much about us at all. I keep waiting, keep holding the topic open, but you remain silent as a mime."

She felt that old reluctance surface again. "We'll talk soon. I promise." Giving a smile, she turned back to the bags. "But right now I'm starved!"

"Don't you ever eat?" Greg asked, letting the subject drop, but she had a feeling it wasn't going to be the last time it would be brought up. From what she'd seen, the man was persistent. She doubted if he would leave this topic alone.

"Not unless you're buying." She unpacked the first paper bag while Greg pulled out the CD player and plugged it in, starting up an Eric Clapton album that was slow and sad and really, really good. As she opened the containers, she realized this wasn't fast-food fare, but had probably been catered from some very elegant restaurant.

"And the chef is…?" she finally asked, looking at the array of opened containers.

"Sierra Restaurant." Greg pulled out two plates, then grabbed some silverware. "They have some of the best food in town."

"I've heard of them," Mary Ellen murmured. She tried to remember the last time she'd eaten out. It had been a very long time ago.

They ate listening to compact discs, their conversation more about the day's activities than anything more personal. Mary was relieved. She wasn't ready for the intensity of a personal topic. It hung in the air between them, prepared to be plucked and discussed, but neither reached for it. Neither wanted the ultimate confrontation that would come of it.

After dinner, Greg gathered the plates while Mary put away the salt, pepper, butter and napkins. She turned to reach for the sponge and was caught in Greg's arms.

"Dance with me," he said, wrapping his arms around her and taking slow and easy steps to the music. B. B. King and Diane Shuur sang a sultry duet about everlasting love, and just listening to it made Mary Ellen want to melt into Greg's strength.

Her head fit perfectly in the hollow of his shoulder as she nestled in his arms. His body melded to hers as he led her slowly, easily around the floor. She'd never felt so secure, so very protected, in her whole life. *Watch it, girl. That sounds like a setup for disaster!*

Mary lifted her head, dancing a little more stiffly than before. She wasn't going to let the sounds of soulful music seduce her. Not this time. This time she would be in control, just like she'd been last night. This time…

"Relax. I don't bite and I'm not on the make. I just want to dance with you."

She looked up at him, but his eyes were closed as he moved her smoothly around the kitchen. "That's all?"

He nodded. "For now."

"And you'll tell me when you're changing your mode?"

"You'll be the first to know." His eyes were still closed, his lashes thicker and longer than a woman's and twice as sexy. It wasn't fair.…

"Okay, then," she said, carefully nestling her

head back onto his shoulder. Her body slowly relaxed, melting against him.

The music ended, but Greg didn't release her.
Instead, he tightened his arms and kissed her
lightly on the temple. Mary didn't move. Her
breath caught in her throat. Tears welled in her
eyes. She'd never been treated so carefully never
felt so treasured, and she wasn't sure how to act
or what to say. Instead, she did nothing and remained silent, reveling in the feelings that almost
overwhelmed her. But her heart overflowed with
love.

Another song began and Mary Ellen burrowed
even further into the warmth of Greg's body.
With her arms wrapped around his neck, she
swayed to the music as if the notes ran through
her veins in perfect harmony.

Greg hugged her to him and they flowed together like liquid. Mary gave a small smile as she
felt his reaction to her nearness. He might still
have some feelings for his ex-wife, but it didn't
stop him from enjoying her femininity.

Stop it, Mary Ellen Gallagher! she told herself.
*You don't know that he's in love with his ex-wife.
You're assuming! And that doesn't count, because it's
your big fear. Not reality!*

Just then, Greg leaned down and kissed her
nose, then her mouth. It started out as just a light
peck, but good intentions…

They stood in the center of her kitchen, surrounded by music. The one dim ceiling bulb

barely gave off enough light to see across the room.

Mary lost herself in Greg's kiss, reveling in the feelings he provoked. When the front doorbell rang, the jarring sound intruded loudly on their intimacy; they both jumped.

"Who's that?" Greg asked, his voice rough with feeling.

Mary gave a shaky laugh. "I haven't answered the door yet, so I don't know."

She flipped on the hall light, then walked to the door on legs that were less than steady. When she answered the door, Greg was just a few feet behind her, encased in shadows.

She was not prepared for her visitor. "Joe!"

Her sandy-haired ex-boyfriend stood under the porch light, looking just as young and vulnerable and boyish as ever. Instead of that familiar rush of yearning she thought she'd feel if this time ever came, she was alarmed and irritated! "What are you doing here?"

"Hi, Mary Ellen. I'm sorry to surprise you, but I need to talk." His hair glittered in the yellow porch light; his expression was sad and drawn. If he was trying to look pathetic, he was succeeding. "I thought about calling but wasn't sure you'd talk to me after the way I behaved, and I need to apologize."

Apologize? She doubted it. "What exactly is it you want?" she asked, her spine straightening, her gaze cold with half-buried anger. "I think it's a little too late for an apology, but if you'd like to donate a check to help defray the wedding expenses I had to pay for, you can send it to me."

"Mary, I was a coward, I know. But if you'll just hear me out…" he said, boyish charm lighting up his eyes.

She remembered that look well; it used to work on her. It was the look she'd fallen in love with. But not now. Not anymore. He'd hurt her more than she could say, and certainly more than she would admit to him or anyone else.

She felt Greg's presence in the hallway. He hadn't come up directly behind her, but she knew he was within earshot. Mary Ellen was thankful—it helped keep her backbone just a little stiffer. "I'm sorry, but this isn't a good time. Call and make an appointment during the day, Joe, and we'll talk then."

"Mary, please," he said, taking a step toward her as if to enter the house.

Suddenly, after more than two years, Mary knew she was rid of this man emotionally. This son of a gun had cost her enough heartache. She really didn't need any more. "Like I said, Joe. Call sometime and we'll discuss this. But right now, I have company."

Joe gave her a disbelieving look, raising her irritation even further. He thought he could weasel his way in. Six months ago, that might have been true, but now it wasn't worth her effort to listen to him. She just plain didn't care anymore. She opened the door fully so he could see Greg standing behind her. "Have a good evening, Joe. Say hello to your wife."

"We're divorcing." His gaze was glued to Greg, assessing, compiling. Challenging. "And you're the cause of it all."

"I had nothing to do with it," Mary Ellen stated through clenched teeth. At last she'd found her anger. "I was the one left at the altar, remember? I was the one who paid the bills and explained the problems to my friends and relatives—and half of yours. If anyone was the cause of your marriage falling apart, Joe, I'd place bets that it was you."

"Unfair," he said. "You left me with a huge telephone bill."

"Be thankful that was all," she retorted. "Not quite enough to split up a marriage you sacrificed me and your all for, is it?"

But the discussion was closed. Greg moved closer and placed a protective arm around her waist. Joe stepped backward.

It must have been a male-animal thing; they had sized each other up and Joe was lacking whatever it took for a confrontation. Of course, he'd never been good at it or he wouldn't have left her without warning for another woman....

"Good night, Joe," she said softly, closing the door with a definite click. She turned and leaned against the wood, facing Greg, her heart hammering in her breast. She didn't know whether she was excited or nervous or...

When Joe's footsteps faded and the car engine

started up, she let out her breath. She was surprised to find she was shaking, and clasped her hands together in front of her.

"So that's him."

Blankly, she gazed up. "What?"

"That's the guy who hurt you so much."

There was no sense in denying it. "Yes."

"He's young and stupid."

She gave a small grin. "And you're not young?"

"Not *that* young, and *never* that stupid."

"How stupid?" she asked. Without thinking, she rested her hands against his chest, feeling the warmth of his skin through his shirt. He felt real and reliable and not capable of doing what Joe had done to her. From the very start Greg had been up-front and willing to discuss whatever made them both easier in this relationship.

But not Joe. From the moment they became involved, he'd been sneaky. And with each sneaky thing he'd done, she'd spiralled closer to zero self-esteem. He had hurt her so deeply she was afraid to check if that old wound had opened again.

Greg covered her hands with his own. "Stupid enough to hurt someone because I couldn't make up my mind what I wanted."

"Everyone's that stupid sometime in their life. Everyone hurts someone, Greg. We're fools if we think otherwise."

"And who did you hurt?"

"A guy in high school who followed me

around like a puppy. I didn't like him and so I ignored him. When he asked me to the prom, I
turned him down as if I'd been insulted."

"On purpose?"

"No, I was too young to handle those kinds of
feelings. Sometimes I think what happened with
Joe and me was payback time for that young
guy."

"You believe the old what-you-reap-you-sow
thing?"

"Yes."

"Well, I don't," he stated flatly. "People get
hurt all the time but that doesn't mean they have
to suffer later for whatever they did. We're all
just human and will err as we learn. Besides, if
that was the case, everyone but the most stupid
would learn their lessons in life and never repeat
all the ugly things we do to each other over and
over. And there would be no murderers or
thieves or nasty people out there. But there are."

She gave a shaky laugh. "You're too philo-
sophical for me."

"Look," Greg said, giving her hands a light
squeeze. His hazel eyes were intense and filled
with conviction. "This is the only life we know.
Right here, right now. The guy who just left was
a jerk. He lost something and now he thinks he
wants it back. He hasn't learned anything except
that at least two women didn't make him happy.
He's still looking for some magic formula, but
the poor jerk doesn't realize it's inside himself.
He may *never* know that. Are you going to take a

chance with him, and with hurting yourself, instead of hurting him by saying no?"

"I don't ever want to see him again," she said, her voice low with the pain she'd not felt earlier.

"But do you still love him?" Greg persisted.

"No." It was true. Her chin came up. "No."

"Is your pride hurt?"

"It was," she admitted, her tight throat finally easing slightly. "But I think his apology just served as the best balm in the world."

Greg smiled, but it wasn't a charming sight. "Good. Then I don't have to beat the pulp out of him."

"Of course not!" Mary Ellen was shocked at his statement. But the idea intrigued her. "Would you have done that?"

"Sure. Big strong men love protecting their women. Don't you know that?"

Mary laughed. He was outrageous. "Joe wouldn't fight for me. He doesn't even *want* me."

"Oh, yes he does, Mary quite contrary." Greg looked somber and just a little angry. "If he hadn't wanted you, he wouldn't have knocked on your door this evening. And not even a jerk takes the chance of being turned down unless he thinks he's wanted or unless there's something he wants enough to take a risk over."

Mary went on tiptoe and kissed his cheek. "I'm thankful you were here."

"Why? Because if I hadn't been here you would have let him in and regretted it later?"

"No, silly. Because now he knows I'm not alone and pining for him."

"Thanks," he said dryly. "It's nice to know I'm a useful substitute."

"You're not a substitute, Greg," she began, but her throat closed and she felt as if she was on the verge of crying. "I'm sorry," she whispered as tears welled in her eyes. "I did use you, and that wasn't fair." She swallowed back the sob that rose from nowhere, but it was too late. Greg heard it.

"Damn," he muttered, encompassing her in his arms and cradling her as is she were a child. "Double damn."

There was no holding on to her composure. If he'd been remote, she would have been, too. But with the least bit of tenderness, she fell apart.

She wasn't even sure why she was crying so heartily. She was certain she didn't love Joe anymore. Looking at him was like looking at a stranger, or someone from another life. Still, his apology had been a soothing balm to her soul and justified all those angry feelings she'd had after their breakup. But most of all, she was certain she didn't love Joe because of the way she felt about Greg.

She loved Greg. Dear sweet heaven, she'd fallen in love with him!

That was *exactly* what she *hadn't* wanted to do! Her sobs became louder.

"It's okay, darlin'," Greg crooned. "That jerk is out of your life now. He won't come back. I guar-

antee it. You don't have to worry about him
again. Understand?"

"I know," she whispered, sounding more like
a diver underwater than a woman in her lover's
arms. "I'm glad. Honest."

"He's no good for you."

"I know."

"You need someone like me."

"I know." Her head popped up. "Wait a minute." Was he patronizing her? She stared into his
eyes, her tears drying up. "I don't *need* anyone."

"We all need someone, Mary. Even you and
me."

"Speak for yourself." She began pulling away,
but he held her captive instead of letting her go.

"Now, wait a minute. Don't go running off unless you're kicking me out. And if you're kicking
me out, you'd better tell me first, and then give
me a damn good reason why."

"Stop cursing," she said automatically, her
mind swirling with emotions and thoughts, none
of them making sense. "And I'm not throwing
you out, I just don't like being restrained any
more than you would."

Carefully, Greg removed his hands. "You're
right. I'm sorry. I just didn't want you to leave
yet."

She looked up at him, wondering what in the
world was wrong with her. She'd just realized
she loved the man, and she was attacking him!

She hadn't done anything that made any sense

so far, so she might as well continue in that vein. "Let's go to bed."

His grin was slow in coming, but it lit up the dim hallway—and her heart. "Lady, now you're talking."

He took her hand and they walked up the stairs together. By moonlight they undressed— slowly, carefully, putting clothing in neat piles. When they climbed into bed, neither touched the other. Each was waiting, waiting, waiting.

Gathering up all her courage, Mary turned toward him and leaned over. She reached out and stroked his chest, slowly slipping the sheet down as she traced his muscles, his ribs, his trim waist. Her palms burned…as did her insides. This was the man she loved, the man she craved. She knew they had problems they'd have to work through, but right now nothing mattered as much as being with him and knowing he wanted to be with her.

"Touch me everywhere," he said, his voice husky. He kept his arms at his sides, giving her the courage to continue.

She felt his hips, his long thigh, then came up on the inside of his legs, finally reaching her goal.

"That's a great 'everywhere,'" he whispered hoarsely.

She picked up his hand and put it in the same place on her own body. "It certainly is," she answered breathlessly.

It was as if she'd turned on a switch. Greg rolled over, taking her prisoner. "And is this a great place?'' he asked, grazing her breasts with his mouth.

"Yes."

"And this?'' he asked, gently kissing her belly button.

"Oh, yes."

"And what about this?'' he asked, his hand moving between her legs slowly, easily, knowing exactly where those tender, sensitive spots were.

"Yes." Her voice was barely audible.

She reached for him, but Greg had moved on. "And this?'' he asked.

But she had nothing more to say. She couldn't speak. Her breath was caught in her throat and could only be released in a sigh....

Their lovemaking was slow and easy, but Mary felt the intensity of one who loves with all her heart and communicates it by touch, by sighs and by suppleness. She couldn't say the words, though. She would probably never do that. This was her only form of communication.

She cried out in ecstasy just as he spilled his seed, holding on to her as if she were the only anchor in a rolling sea. She clung to him, giving him what she could of her love, sharing the most intimate play of her body. She hoped he knew that the gift came from her heart. She prayed he would understand.

She loved him. There was no doubt, no choice anymore. It was true—a fact.

Late that night, curled against him with his hand stroking her side as she fell asleep, she dreamed that he loved her, too.

Of course, it was only a dream.

8

MARY ELLEN WAS WORKING hard on new assignments that Edie had procured, and the prospect of future business looked good.

She kept herself as busy as she could, which was imperative if she was going to make a success of her business. At the same time, she spent the nights with Greg, making love with him until she fell asleep at his side, only to repeat it all the next day and night.

She was exhausted.

Every morning she rose just before six o'clock with Greg, and every evening they stayed up until after midnight. As soon as he left, she would spring into work mode.

Greg had asked her to wait until they completed a major shipment for a project in the North Sea before she started filming in the plant. She agreed. It was only a two-week delay, and by that time the plant floor would be back to business as usual and the pressure would be off. A few smiles for the camera wouldn't be so hard to come by.

A constant stream of little jobs—weddings, a small commercial for another jewelry company, a test film for a pianist—came through her doors these days, and for that she was thankful. Now if she could just get enough sleep so she wasn't walking around fuzzy headed all day!

"You've got to do something about your yawning," Edie commented one morning. "It's catching."

"I'm not—" Mary Ellen yawned "—yawning." She plopped down in the easy chair next to Edie's desk, exhausted. "I give up. I'm so pooped I can't even think anymore!"

"I know," Edie commiserated cheerily. "This love stuff is exhausting, isn't it? All this and work, too. I remember and I'm jealous."

"Does it show?"

"Oh," Edie asked innocently, "was I not supposed to notice the two coffee cups and empty packets of sugar—which you don't use—by the coffeepot? Am I not supposed to see the blue circles under your eyes? Or what about the fact that you've lost weight these past two weeks? Or that you sometimes sneak upstairs to take a nap in the afternoon, then come down dressed and made up as if company was coming?"

"Good grief," Mary Ellen said disgustedly. "I've left a bigger trail than Gretel, haven't I?"

"You could say so. But at least it's a happy trail," Edie said, closing the file she'd been working on. "So far you've been able to juggle both your career and the man in your life. But I think it's starting to catch up with you."

Mary Ellen yawned again. "Maybe so. It's ten

o'clock in the morning and I've got to get some sleep."

"Go for it. You've got one appointment today I can reschedule. The dubbing can wait a few days—there's no rush. Why not take a day off? Sleep. Tomorrow morning you'll be filming at Greg's factory, and then you have to shoot the local clock shop's television commercials."

"Oh, Lord, I'm tired just thinking about it." Mary stood and made her way to the stairs. "I'll be down in a little while, but right now I've got to take a nap before I fall flat on my face."

"You go, girl," Edie stated, reaching for another file. "I'll just sit here and bill all these people and wait for them to send lovely checks in the mail. Pretty soon I'll have a raise and an assistant, and life will be wonderful."

"I'm the one going to sleep, but she's the one daydreaming," Mary muttered as she headed upstairs.

Edie heard her and laughed. "I'm married, which means we don't have to have marathon nights of lovemaking. We just sit and stare at each other as we remember what it was like to be in your spot. Or at least we used to until Grant got his new second job." Her voice was just a little bitter.

"What fun."

Edie's voice carried all the way up the stairs. "You'll see when you've been together awhile."

Mary was too tired to give the answer she knew she should. She didn't know how long it would last, but she prayed she and Greg would continue as a couple for a long time. She loved him and wanted to be with him for as long as she could.

Reaching her bedroom, she collapsed on the bed and closed her eyes. Within seconds she was sound asleep and dreaming of all the possibilities....

When she awoke, she was in Greg's arms, nuzzling his chest.

Mary blinked once, then blinked again. "Greg?"

"Were you expecting someone else in your bed?" he asked, a tinge of humor in his tone.

"I was dreaming about you," she said, a smile lifting the corners of her mouth as she closed her eyes and curled back into him. "It was just before dawn and we were making love."

"Don't tell me or I'll lose my resolve," he said, giving the soft spot at the base of her throat a kiss. "Then we'd wind up staying here and making mad, passionate love all night instead of dining at a fine restaurant and enjoying lobster and steak with a good bottle of wine."

Her eyes opened and she stared at him suspiciously. "You're taking me out?"

"Yes."

"Why?"

"Because I feel as if I'm hiding you away from the public, which I am. And that's not right. You deserve better. You—we—deserve a night on the town."

Her eyes widened. "I—we do?"

He nodded. "Besides, you owe it to me for turning me down the last time I asked."

Mary leaned back and stared at him. He was wearing slacks, an open-necked shirt and a fabulous sports jacket. And he smelled like a sexy million bucks.

"After dinner, we're going to my place for a change."

"I have to work in the morning," she warned him.

"So do I. Remember?" He leaned back against the headboard. "And if I'm not mistaken, you're supposed to be at my place of work tomorrow, too."

She got the message. He'd spent every night in the past two weeks at her home. It seemed only fair that she do the traveling on occasion.

"I have a load of cameras to take with me," she warned.

"Cut down on the load and do the preliminary filming tomorrow instead."

"How do you know what I should do?"

"Because I did my homework before I hired you and found out your regular routine."

She looked up at him, a mischievous glint in her eye. "So you want me to dress in some sexy little number that will make you proud to spend a fortune on dinner with the world watching. You want me to pack my suitcase for business tomorrow and make sure that all my supplies are ready to roll for beginning filming, and you want me to be charming at the same time. Is that right?"

He smiled contentedly. "Perfect. I knew you'd get the hang of it."

"How much time do I have until dinner reservations?" she asked, knowing he'd made them or he'd be stripped of his clothes and in bed with her.

"About two hours." He ran his hand up and down her arm, his touch both soothing and erotic at the same time. "No more."

Not wanting to show just how much his touch meant to her, she left the bed and started rummaging in the closet. "I can do it if I hurry," she muttered to herself, dragging out a garment bag, then reaching for her cosmetic case. "Meanwhile, if you want to check on the wiring of that socket in the office, I'd appreciate it. The one closest to Edie's desk isn't working."

"Work, work, work," he grumbled as he stood and tucked in his shirt, but he was still smiling. "I hope you're worth it."

"Of course I am," she declared. "Or you wouldn't be here to begin with." She pulled out a pair of new hose and dumped them in the garment bag. "I'll be down in an hour. There's a beer and a bottle of wine in the fridge. Take your choice, and pour me a glass of wine while you're at it, would you?"

"You've turned into a bossy little thing, haven't you?"

"I always was." Mary Ellen pulled her little

black dress from the closet and tossed it on the bed. Then she chose a peach-colored suit to wear for tomorrow. A minute of deliberation was all it took to change her mind and pull out a pale gray pantsuit, instead. It was easier working in slacks than a skirt. Looking over her selection, she chose a camp shirt of Irish green silk. "You just never noticed before."

Greg watched her, almost able to see the thought processes whirring. "Great. Not only bossy, but logical and faultfinding, too." He left the room, but not before giving her a kiss on the back of her neck and a light pat on her rump. "Back in twenty minutes with your wine."

A giggle bubbled up, but she was wise enough to keep it to herself. She felt so wonderfully happy. Greg not only wanted her, he wanted to show her off in public. It felt like a piece of heaven had dropped in her lap. She'd been so afraid to grasp and hold it to her heart. But no more.

It was time to take a chance.

Although she wasn't sure that Greg loved her any more than Joe had, she was absolutely certain of one thing. She loved Greg. Everything else was out of her hands. Nevertheless, she wanted this relationship to work more than she'd ever wanted anything in her life, and if it was up to her, it would. But it wasn't up to her alone; Greg had to want it, too.

She said a quick prayer and crossed her fingers.

It took forty-five minutes to shower, do her hair with a curling iron, put on makeup she didn't normally use, and then pack her clothes and cosmetics.

Halfway through, Greg strolled into the bathroom with one of her best crystal wineglasses filled with red wine. She turned to kiss his cheek, but he was gone. The small napkin under the glass had a note scribbled on it: "I miss you. Hurry."

When she came downstairs, Mary Ellen found Greg sitting in the office and watching a program on the TV set up to show clients her work. He looked up from the easy chair near Mary Ellen's desk and his eyes widened. "Good grief, you are gorgeous," he said, his gaze warming her from head to toe.

"Thank you," she answered simply. "Does that mean you won't be embarrassed to be seen with me?"

"That's what it means, all right." He stood and glanced at his watch. "And you're an hour and fifteen minutes early." He rolled his eyes to the ceiling. "What more could any man ask?"

"Camera equipment isn't packed yet," Mary warned, dropping her garment bag by the front door. "I'll be done in about fifteen minutes if everything is ready."

"Can I help?"

"No, thanks," she said as she walked into her equipment closet.

It was half an hour before she came out. Three

small still cameras, two battery packs and one video camera were packed inside a large, hard-sided suitcase on wheels. "Now I'm ready." Mary picked up her purse and turned to face him. "Come on, big boy. You promised to buy me lobster and steak and I won't settle for less."

"Yes, ma'am." Greg picked up the garment bag, then rolled the camera case out to the car while Mary set the alarm.

Half an hour later they were seated at a table in one of the city's trendiest restaurants. Mary Ellen was glad she'd worn her best "little black dress." It might not have a designer label, but at least it didn't put her to shame. In fact, she was feeling pretty proud of the way she looked tonight.

They ordered from a waiter who knew Greg by name, which made Mary a little uneasy. How many times did people pay extravagant tabs here before they were known by name? It went without saying that he'd probably brought others here, both men and women. It also went without saying that there was a wide financial gap between her and Greg. And where there was a money gap, there was usually a social gap, too.

As if to illustrate the point, a well-dressed gentleman halted beside their table. His gray hair shone in the recessed lighting. "Greg! How great to see you!"

Greg chuckled as he stood and shook the distinguished man's outstretched hand. "Mark, how the hell are you and where have you been?"

"Spent the last two months on the coast of Italy."

"Well, you sure look rested," Greg said. Mary thought so, too. The older man's tan was the perfect tone, coppery without looking weathered.

"Did nothing but lay up like a fattening hog, and I don't feel guilty at all," he stated. "I was fed by the best chefs and wined by the best local vineyards. I told you, you needed to join us."

"Who went?"

He named off several couples. "Jack and Joyce had their sailboat in the Mediterranean, and we played on that for a week or so."

Greg grinned. "Some of us have to work for a living."

"Not you! I've seen your financial statement, remember?" He glanced at Mary Ellen as if seeing her for the first time. Suddenly ignoring Greg, he held out his hand to her. "Hello, I'm Mark Hawthorne, an old friend of this workaholic."

She placed her hand in his. "I'm Mary Ellen Gallagher." Instead of shaking her hand, he kissed it, holding it much longer than necessary. She gave a gentle tug to get it back. But there was a small part of her that delighted as much in the grand gesture as the frown it brought to Greg's face. She didn't want him to be jealous, but it wouldn't hurt him to be a little concerned....

"Great taste," Mark murmured to Greg.

"And not on the menu," Greg said in return.

"Mary is the video photographer our company hired for a new pump commercial."

Mark's eyes lit up. "Oh, really? What an interesting occupation for a woman."

Mary laughed. "It's an interesting occupation for anyone, Mr. Hawthorne."

He grimaced. "Ouch, please don't call me Mr. Hawthorne. That's my father and he's not here right now. Although the old buzzard's been known to show up in the most unlikely places, with the most likely escorts."

"And you're alone tonight," Greg assumed.

Mark smiled. "Yes."

Mary knew where this was leading. Mark wanted to eat dinner with them. She waited to see what Greg would do. It was an interesting situation, and the byplay between the two friends was intriguing.

But Greg was certainly up to the challenge. She should have known. He gave a sympathetic shake of his head. "What a shame. You really need to find a girl, Mark. And as I've just found the woman I want to spend the evening with, I'll talk to you again on Monday morning."

Mark made a face that Mary was sure worked with others. "That's not nice."

"No, but it's necessary if I'm to have Mary's company all to myself. Besides, I didn't get a chance to take a vacation. This is mine."

"Brains and beauty, too," Mark murmured. "I may have need of a video myself. Do you have a card?"

Mary looked regretful. "I'm sorry, I didn't bring one. However, I'm listed in the directory." She gave him the name of her company. "Or you can call information."

Mark looked as triumphant as Greg looked angry. "I'll call," he promised. "See you later, Greg. Have a great vacation."

When Greg sat back down, he took a deep breath. "If I continue taking you out in public, I'm going to have to fight off the men. I can see that now."

"You're exaggerating."

Greg shook his head. "You're new to this part of the jungle, and there are different rules here. I don't like men like Mark taking advantage of you. He's a flirt and doesn't treat women as nicely as he should unless they're married or with someone else."

"I run a business for profit, not fun. It's part of the job to drum up prospects." Mary leaned forward, her arms crossed on the table. "Don't you think I can take care of myself?"

"Like I said, not in this jungle."

Mary placed her napkin on the table and pushed back her chair. "Well, you're wrong."

Greg stood up with her. "And you're leaving just because I hinted you might not be able to handle yourself?"

She gave a husky laugh. "Not likely. I want to eat steak and lobster until my seams pop. But right now, I'm going to the ladies' room. I'll be back by the time our salads arrive," she promised. But his words had put a twinkle in her eye and a bounce in her step as she walked toward the back of the restaurant.

GREG WATCHED MARY walk off. That shape-hugging little black dress was also short, with a flirty little flair at the hem that accented the de-lightfully feminine sway of her hips. He felt that sway all the way down to his toes, raising his heartbeat several notches.

He was here with the best-looking woman in the restaurant. What more could he ask for?

He didn't know, but something had been eat-ing at him lately. He was happy, but he wasn't content—he didn't have that feeling of every-thing being perfect with Mary. And he wanted it. He wanted it badly.

"So you finally decided it was time to have a little fun and get out of your office," a familiar woman's voice said.

Greg looked up and met his ex-wife's gaze. "Well, I'll be damned," he replied with a smile. "Thinking good thoughts can manifest real vi-sions."

Janet stood in front of him as she held on to some man's arm. Having lots of money, she had long ago shed the necessity of little black dresses that went everywhere. She was in a bright rose red dress that did flattering things to her figure. "You always were a charmer, Greg." She looked pointedly at the place setting next to him. "Where and who is your date?"

"It's Mary Ellen Gallagher and she's in the rest room."

Janet's eyes lit with mirth. "Wonderful," she said, looking mischievous. "Funny, I'm headed that way myself." Before either man could stop her, she had given her date a quick kiss on the cheek and turned. "I'll be right back."

Greg's heart sank a little. He forced a smile he was sure looked more like a grimace and motioned to Mary's chair. "You may as well sit down. This might take some time."

The other man stuck out his hand, going through the ritual of being civilized. "Janet tells me you're her partner and ex-husband. I'm Tom Hendricks."

Greg didn't stand but he did shake hands. It wasn't this guy's fault Janet was impulsive. "What do you do, Tom?"

"I'm a doctor. A pediatrician."

"Oh, really?"

"Yes. As a matter of fact, I saw your son two days ago. A nice kid."

"He's okay, isn't he?" Greg frowned. Janet hadn't said anything about their son being ill. Besides, she never would have left him if he was....

"He had a headache and a stuffy nose. I wrote it off to allergies. Every kid is allergic to something blooming."

Tom took Mary's seat gingerly, as if he would jump up at the first sign of trouble or women, whichever came first. Greg relaxed. This guy wasn't any more sure about how to act or what to say than Greg had been when Janet first began introducing him to her dates. Poor son of a gun.

They talked about Jason for a while, and other things: weather, places to eat, new shows and sports. But all the time they both kept an eye on the well-lit hallway leading to the bathrooms. Where in the hell were the women and what were they finding to talk about?

"BUT THEN, it's like father, like son," Janet said, pulling out a lip brush and beginning the tedious process of lining her lips. "You know. They have that gene that pops up just at puberty that eliminates all the good things you've done to raise them. Instead hormones attack their brains and make them suddenly believe that women aren't quite as smart or powerful or right as God made men."

Mary laughed. "I've seen that gene in action. It puts a glaze in some men's eyes that makes them see all women in a bedroom or a kitchen—and it has nothing to do with remodeling fever!"

"That's the one," Janet confirmed, filling in her already perfect lips. "Well, Greg never had that gene bloom full force. He had me to separate the weeds from the wildflowers ever since we were in elementary school. But once in a while, it doesn't do any harm to remind him just how silly the gene is, just in case he wants to develop it in our son."

Mary Ellen snapped her little black bag closed. Her smile slowly faded away as she realized the import of Janet's words. For just a fleeting moment, she'd forgotten that this woman was Greg's ex-wife and the mother of his child. But now she was reminded, and the awkwardness of the situation struck her. She was standing in the bathroom of a well-known restaurant discussing the merits of men with the ex-wife of the man she was dating—the man she was in love with!

Janet must have been able to read her mind. "Look, just because Greg and I are divorced doesn't mean I have to hate him or vice versa. He's a wonderful guy in so many ways or I wouldn't have dated him for twice as long as we were married. And no matter what happens, he's the father of my son. How bad can he be?"

Mary leaned against the counter as she stared intently at Janet. "Then why did you divorce him?"

Janet did the same thing—leaning her hip against the counter and looking Mary fully in the eye. "Because he deserves someone who cares about him in a loving, passionate way." She gave a little sigh. "And I deserve it, too. He would have stayed with me forever and ignored all the signs that he was unhappy. But I couldn't. We'd been together for so long that it never dawned on him there was something missing. He wasn't happy, just comfortable. I wasn't happy, either." She smiled. "No matter how many times I tried to explain it, he brushed my emotions off, telling me it was just my imagination. But it wasn't. We didn't have that real, male-female love that makes two people feel connected and everything to each other."

Mary nodded. "But Greg still feels that way toward you."

"No, he doesn't." Janet's eyes were smoky with a momentary sadness. "He just hasn't realized how lucky he is that I let him go." She grinned slowly, and her whole face lit up again. "But he will, eventually. Meanwhile, can we be friends?"

"I'd like that," Mary Ellen answered honestly.

"Great," Janet said. "But right now, I've got a very special guy outside who's probably talking to Greg about sports. Neither one of them really enjoys that type of conversation, so we'd better go rescue them."

"Women to the rescue?" Mary said with a laugh.

"But of course," Janet answered complacently. "What else is new? We're always good at that— and that's why women should rule the world."

"I've got my Superwoman cape on. We might as well do something to help mankind tonight."

As they walked back into the dining area, Mary realized Janet had been right. Neither man was capable of hiding his relief at seeing his date emerge unscathed from the dim recesses of the ladies' room.

As Mary smiled at the man she loved, she wished she didn't like his ex-wife so much. It made it harder to believe that Greg wasn't still in love with her.

9

GREG UNLOCKED HIS DOOR and stood to one side. Mary Ellen walked in and stared. It was without doubt the most beautiful condominium she'd ever been in. Although the wide foyer was a single story, it opened into a two-story great room that encompassed more space than both floors of her home. To the right was a kitchen with a wraparound bar separating it from the dining area. One massive window filled the entire outer wall; copper- and cream-colored bricks covered the inner wall, fireplace and an archway that she assumed led to the bedroom wing.

The furniture shouted luxurious comfort. Deep-cushioned, forest green leather sofas flanked the fireplace and a huge Monetlike painting above it. The room was decorated in greens, pale yellows, rose and gold, which drew the eye outside to the balcony, where pots of trees and flowers bloomed in an artfully arranged container garden.

Mary stepped to the glass doors and looked out. "Tomatoes? You've got tomatoes growing up here?"

Greg dropped his keys on an antique rolltop desk and walked up behind her, pulling her back against him as they stared out at the night sky. Below them Houston was laid out like a magic carpet awash with color and light. It had to be one of the prettiest skylines she'd ever seen.

Greg's arms tightened, bringing her closer. Again that treasured feeling came over her. "Yes, those are tomatoes. Two different kinds. I've also got some cantaloupe, cabbage and several herbs." He kissed her ear. "And before you ask, yes, I use them. And what I don't use, Janet does."

Janet. Mary Ellen wished she had the ability to distance herself from Greg's ex-wife the way he seemed to. She gave a sigh.

Greg misunderstood. "Tired?"

"A little."

"Let's go to bed," he suggested, but neither moved. With his arms resting just under her breasts, they stared out at the skyline. A shooting star arched across the midnight blue sky. "Look," Greg said very quietly, pointing.

"Beautiful," she murmured. And she silently repeated her own dream of happiness—of owning a successful business, having a man who loved her and children—lots of children.

"Are you making a wish?"

"No. Are you?"

"Yes. I'm making a wish and a plan." His voice was soft, but filled with the conviction of someone who knew exactly what he wanted. He nuzzled her ear. "And you're part of it."

"Part of your wish or part of your plan?"

"Both."

Very slowly, Mary Ellen turned and wrapped her arms around his neck. Her fingers twined in his hair, feeling the silkiness of it. "Gregory Torrance, if you don't make love to me right now, I'll be forced to leave and dream alone in my lonely bed. I think I'll go crazy if you don't kiss me right away."

His smile was slow and easy and sexy as hell. The light in his hazel eyes pierced her with heat. "I can't have that on my conscience, can I?"

"Not if you know what's good for you." She kissed his throat, the underside of his jaw, the curve of his smile—everywhere but his mouth. Just as his arms tightened with impatience, the doorbell rang. Greg ignored it. "Someday soon you'll tell me about your dreams?"

"Someday," she promised. But it would be a very long time, maybe never.

The doorbell pealed again. "Damn," he muttered, finally letting her go. As soon as he opened the door Mary Ellen heard Janet's voice, sounding high and filled with tension. "Jason has a high fever and it won't come down."

Greg's response was no-nonsense. "When did it start?"

"This afternoon. But when I put him to bed, it seemed to be coming down. Tom even checked him and thought everything was fine and normal for a boy who had the sniffles."

Greg's voice turned sharp. "You should have told me. I thought we agreed one of us would stay with him when he wasn't feeling well."

"He didn't seem to be ill. We thought he had an allergy."

Mary walked into the hallway, but stopped abruptly when she saw a worried Janet shifting a whimpering young boy into Greg's arms.

Carrying his son, Greg walked right by Mary Ellen and disappeared into the first room off the hallway.

Janet followed, not really paying attention to Mary Ellen's presence until she came even with her. Her expression was one of regret. "Oh, Mary, I'm sorry. I didn't mean to ruin your evening."

"I know," Mary Ellen said. "Is there anything I can do?"

Once more, Janet was focused on her son as she followed Greg into the room. "No. Thanks."

Mary stood in the doorway and watched the scenario in front of her. Greg's bedroom was beautifully masculine. It had a slanted ceiling and one wall of glass that had the same view as the living area. The bed was covered with a tailored spread in blacks, browns and whites. Greg's son was stretched out there, his thin legs moving restlessly as he whimpered. He held his dad's hand as if it were a magic amulet.

"Where's Tom now?"

"He dropped me off and left directly for the airport. He's on his way to Dallas for a medical conference. He won't be back for three days."

With his other hand, Greg reached for the

phone by the side of his bed and quickly dialed a number.

"Amanda? Greg here. Sorry to bother you so late, but my son is running a high fever and complaining that his joints hurt. Can you come up and check him for me?" She must have said yes, because his next words were, "Thanks, the front door is open."

Janet soothed her son's brow with a wet cloth. "Another friend?"

"My golfing buddy."

Janet must have understood. She gave a tight nod.

Mary stood still, listening to the byplay and feeling completely invisible. The vignette unfolding in front of her was one that must have been played a hundred times since their son's birth. Both consoled the boy while keeping a united front for him. Both loved and worried and prayed for him to be well. That same vignette would be replayed time after time in the future, too. For as long as they lived, their son would be their focal point. And with a focal point like that, it might be that they could rediscover the attraction they'd once had for each other.

And Mary Ellen would have it no other way.

But there was a part of her that ached to know that feeling of comforting and caring for a child. And to have a partner who felt the depth of feeling toward his offspring in the same way. It had to be wonderful.

Suddenly she wished she was pregnant with Greg's child.

No! No! No!

The front door closed with a solid click and Mary turned, then stepped out of the way of the self-assured brunette with a medical bag who made her way to the bedside.

As Greg stood to allow the doctor closer to Jason, Mary Ellen caught his eye. "I'm leaving," she mouthed, and he shook his head. But there was no sense in staying. It would be a late night for all of them, and Mary would only be in the way. She walked to the living room, grabbed her purse and headed for the door.

Greg beat her to it. "Mary, I'm so sorry."

"Please," she protested. "Jason comes first."

"This isn't the way I wanted the evening to end."

"I know. Take care and let me know how everything comes out."

His gaze was already darting back to the bedroom door as he pulled some money from his pants pocket. "Take this. Juan can get you a taxi downstairs."

She leaned forward and gave him a kiss on the cheek. "Thanks. And don't worry. He'll be fine," she said in a low voice. "I'll talk to you tomorrow." Without waiting for his answer, she brushed by him and walked out the door.

Greg had no recourse but to help his son, and she understood that. Jason had looked so small and helpless, so young and sweet. But the picture of Greg and Janet, their heads bent together in concern over their child, was one Mary Ellen would never forget.

She felt an overwhelming sense of loneliness.

THE NEXT MORNING Mary Ellen awoke feeling as if she'd been drugged. It took a minute to remember the night before, and when she did, depression set in. To top it all off, she was due at Greg's factory this morning.

She drank a cup of coffee as she listened to the messages from yesterday. Edie usually kept track of all this, but had taken yesterday afternoon off. Mary wasn't sure how things were going in Edie's private life, but it was apparent lately that there were a few problems. For her friend's sake, she hoped they worked out well.

There were several calls asking for information on wedding films, which she normally didn't do unless she had nothing else scheduled. There were two calls from her bank asking for a callback, and one from her camera vendor.

"Ms. Gallagher, please call immediately or we will have to confiscate our video equipment within the week. This is your official notification. Please be at our office before noon on Monday with three payments, or we will no longer be doing business."

She stood stock-still, not even breathing. What had happened? With Greg's check, she had paid all the bills, bought a new dubber with cash, given Edie a bonus plus back pay and had set aside one more payment on the equipment. Then she'd given Edie the checkbook to pay whatever miscellaneous bills straggled in. What had gone wrong?

Quickly she dialed Edie's house, but there was no answer. Hoping Edie would be at work before she had to leave, Mary Ellen began getting dressed, only to realize she'd left her garment bag at Greg's home. It took another fifteen minutes to decide what to wear that looked businesslike and still enabled her to move around easily.

Once dressed, she stalled. Where was Edie? After waiting another fifteen minutes, Mary Ellen knew she'd have to call from the factory. There wasn't any time left. She'd left her equipment at Greg's, but it wasn't essential today, anyway. She could get a good overview and go back to film another day.

She called Greg's home, but there was no answer. She left a message about the equipment, asking him to bring it to the office with him when he could.

Leaving a note for Edie, Mary Ellen drove away, her head spinning with everything that had happened in the past twenty-four hours. No matter how positive she tried to be, her depression remained.

Greg wasn't at work, his secretary said. Neither was Janet. They had phoned in from the hospital, where Jason had been admitted last night. They would both be out of the office all day.

Mary called her answering machine, hoping to hear Greg's voice letting her know what was going on. He hadn't phoned. Just as confounding was that Edie hadn't arrived at the office yet, either.

Greg's secretary assigned Keith, an older engineer who looked as if he was ready to retire, to escort her around and explain the workings. Despite her problems, Mary found it interesting.

They entered a room where five men and women sat at desks punching up screen after screen on computers, or searching through large catalogs as they spoke to customers.

"This is the expeditor room. Once an order is given to a sales rep for a pump to be made, staff here follow the pump's progress, making sure there aren't any holdups or snags. They let the client know what's going on every step of the way, and specify extra parts they'll need to order coordinate their current system with the new pump. That way there aren't any surprises or delays." He grinned. "In theory."

"Of course," Mary said, already picturing several shot angles.

They went to another area with banks of computers. "Each pump is made separately and by special order, out of components that can handle the chemicals it will deliver," Keith explained. "This is where the plans are drawn so it can be built into the final product. I give the specs— specifications—and these auto-cad designers draw it up on computers. Then I okay it, and they send it on to the fabrication plant.''

"What happens if there's a problem?''

"I take it to Greg and we discuss it. Sometimes I take it to Janet. It depends on what the problem is.''

He continued leading Mary Ellen around, explaining what their company was all about. His knowledge was great, but his attitude was definitely patronizing. She'd just about had enough of it when he led her back to Greg's secretary.

Mary held out her hand. "Thanks, Keith. I appreciate all your help and information.''

"No problem. It's hard work escorting a beautiful woman around the plant, but I understand that someone has to do it. I'm just glad I could explain it in words you could understand, little lady.''

She was so proud of herself for not flinching. It wasn't meant as a derogatory statement, but that didn't mean it wasn't said to keep her in her place—below him. "Well, you did a thorough job. I'll be sure to mention your devotion to your job to Greg when I see him.''

Keith looked a little startled. "I, uh, I didn't mean to…''

So he had known he was being patronizing. "I know," she said. "I didn't mean it, either.'' But she felt a little better for making the point.

The next four hours she spent with a small still camera in hand, wandering through the facility and taking pictures that would help her in setting up a sequence of filming with the video camera. After that she would come up with the narrative and begin piecing the program together.

She tried reaching Edie one more time, without luck, then continued with the photo shoot. Lost in the process, she discovered it was after three o'clock when she finally finished and let Greg's secretary know she was leaving.

Now that her work was over, she could concentrate on the worries at hand.

What had happened to Greg's son?

What had happened to her bank account and checks?

Where was Edie?

When Mary Ellen reached home, Edie still wasn't there. With a tired sigh, Mary punched the recorder and listened to the messages.

"Mary, this is Edie. Grant landed in jail on a driving-while-intoxicated charge and I've been with the attorney all day trying to get him out. I won't be able to get back to you until he's out and safe. Maybe another day or so, I don't know." Her voice was so distraught, so tense. "Anyway, I'll talk to you soon, but I'll have to call you, 'cause I won't be home until who knows when."

"Great," Mary muttered, frustrated both for Edie and for herself. "This isn't the best week I've had, but it better be the last bad week."

She glanced through the mail, finding several duns from creditors there. What the heck was going on? Suddenly, she realized that along with the duns were notices from her bank. She slit one open and felt a chill spilling down her spine. Three good-sized checks had bounced.

Mary ripped open the next envelope. Two more checks had bounced.

She continued to rip open envelopes. When they were all open she sat in the desk chair and stared. Altogether, seventeen checks had bounced, adding bank charges totaling over four hundred dollars.

She was stunned. Her mind whirled in circles. What was happening? She called the bank's twenty-four-hour number and quickly punched in her account number, then her password. She listened to her balance, a negative, then punched the button to hear her deposits. Greg's company check deposit wasn't listed. It had never made it to the bank. But the checks she'd made out to all her creditors had.

What had happened to the deposit? Mary thought back. Edie was supposed to have taken it to the bank before last week—on the same day the first of these payments were mailed out.

When the phone rang, she was so lost in thought she jumped. Greg's voice sounded even more tired than she was jumpy. "Hi, darlin', I'm sorry I wasn't at work today to see you. How did things go?"

"Fine. Keith showed me around and I got some great shots. I'll work up an order sometime tomorrow." She sounded friendly yet business-like. Good. She could barely concentrate on the conversation. The bank's notices kept flashing through her thoughts. "How is your son doing?"

"He's in the hospital still, but it's looking a lot better. He had the flu and it settled in his lungs in just a few short hours, then he became dehydrated and went into a light coma. It scared the hell out of Janet and me."

She heard the fear in his voice and her heart reached out to him. "I'm so sorry. When will he be able to return home?"

"The doctor says tomorrow or the next day. I came home to get cleaned up. Then I'll go back to the hospital and let Janet do the same. She'll spend the night there and I'll go to work in the morning, then we'll spell each other again."

Janet and Greg. Together. Their child. Mary Ellen's automatic response was as childish as any she'd ever had. Here she was, dreaming it was *her* child with Greg. *They* were the concerned ones, not Janet.

Suddenly she felt petty. This was the way it was when you were in love with a man who already had children. Children came first. Period.

And it was *supposed* to be that way. She felt rotten for thinking otherwise. "If there's anything I can do to help, please call me."

"How about a cup of coffee in the morning?" he asked. "I can stop by on my way to work. I'll bring your equipment and your luggage."

Her heart skipped a beat. "What time?"

"Nine o'clock."

"I'll see you then," she promised. "Meanwhile, get some sleep. You sound terrible."

"Just what every man wants to hear," he teased. "Just when he needs her lovin' the most, his woman thinks he sounds awful instead of sexy."

She warmed all over at being called "his woman." It might not be the most liberated thing to be called, but it felt good anyway. "Isn't that just like a woman?"

He gave a deep, rich chuckle. "See you in the morning. Sweet dreams."

"I plan on it," she said. "Sweet dreams."

After Mary hung up the phone, she hugged herself. Even though Greg was in the middle of a crisis, he cared enough to call. Happiness bubbled up inside her at that thought.

Maybe he cared enough to…

"Don't even think it, Gallagher," she said aloud. She had enough problems to worry about right now.

Flipping through her phone file, she found Edie's number and dialed. The answering machine came on and she left a message for Edie to call as soon as possible.

With the undeveloped film from today's shoot in her hand, she headed for the darkroom. It was going to be a long night. She might as well make the best use of it.

THE FOLLOWING MORNING, Mary Ellen was ready and waiting for Greg. Her photos were dry from

developing the night before, and she laid them
on the large table and played with their order
while she waited. She'd even put some cinnamon buns in the oven in anticipation of Greg's
visit. Their yeasty aroma wafted through the
kitchen, reminding her of the first time they'd
met.

She prayed that Edie would call and tell her
what was going on with the check. She'd called
the bank, which confirmed that the deposit
hadn't been made and the checks were bouncing,
and no, they were sorry, but an interim loan was
not possible. She already owed them several
thousand dollars.

She'd called Greg's secretary and asked if the
check had cleared. The secretary was looking
into it and would call back.

Mary was waiting by the phone when Greg
walked in, obviously tired and drawn. He was
dressed casually in slacks and a pullover shirt,
with loafers that looked as if they were custom-
made for him.

"Hello, beautiful," he said, taking her into his
arms and holding her close. She rested her head
against his chest and heard the heavy thud of his
heartbeat. It was so comforting, so secure in a
world that seemed tenuous at best right now.

She pulled away and took his hand, leading
him to the love seat against the wall. She sat him
down and curled up next to him. "Now, talk to
me," she said softly. "Tell me what's going on."

"Well, Jason is still in the hospital and he'll be

there for a while. He's feeling much better, but they can't seem to get rid of his fever, and until they do he can't go home. Janet is fit to be tied. She refuses to leave him for more than an hour or so at a time." He gave a heavy sigh. "I can't blame her, but now that he's out of the woods, there's no sense both of us staying there twenty-four hours a day, so I'm going to go to work and drive other people crazy."

"Did you get much sleep last night?" she asked, gently pressing his head back and rubbing his temples.

He closed his eyes. "None. I couldn't. But I think I dozed a little. I kept thinking of Jason, then work, then you and then Jason again. I couldn't seem to focus on one thing at a time."

He was worn to a frazzle. She felt his limbs settle into the cushion, and continued to soothingly rub his forehead, temples and cheekbones. Greg gave another sigh, his arm tightening on her waist. After a few minutes, Mary Ellen leaned close to his ear. "Are you hungry?"

Her answer was heavy breathing, but not the kind that raised her pulse rate. Greg was asleep.

She had already turned the oven off, the coffeepot was fine and there was nothing she could do until Greg's secretary or Edie called her with news on the check.

With a contented smile, Mary Ellen rested her head on his chest and closed her eyes. It felt wonderful to lie in the arms of the man she loved. For just a little while, he held off the rest of the world and its problems for her, just as she did for him. Her last thought before dozing off was that this was what love was all about.

Her dreams were sunny and light, with love the focal point. In them she was laughing and taking shots of something she had always wanted to photograph—although she didn't know what it was. Greg was laughing with her, his expression full of fun and optimism and love of life—and her. They were enjoying life as it was meant to be—she knew because her inner voice told her so.

When the phone rang, Greg's arm tightened and she frowned. It took a minute to realize it wasn't the fire alarm, but the call she'd been waiting for. She grabbed the receiver.

It was Greg's secretary. "I'm sorry, Ms. Gallagher, but that check hasn't cleared yet."

At least it hadn't been cashed. That meant it wasn't stolen. "Thanks, I appreciate it. I'll get hold of my secretary and find out what happened."

"Please do. We can deduct the cost of a stop payment and cut you another one if necessary."

When Mary hung up, Greg was sitting up and rubbing his neck. "What's the matter?"

"Not a thing."

"Don't lie, Mary." He might have been sleepy, but he wasn't dopey. "That's not like you."

She held her breath for a moment, wondering where to start, then decided to spill all. "When I got your deposit on the film, I gave it to Edie and wrote a bunch of checks, including her bonus and paycheck. Then a few days ago creditors started calling about their bounced checks. When I phoned the bank, they said there had been no deposit made, but that Edie had cashed her checks immediately, wiping out my account balance. Then I called your secretary, and it turns out the check was never cashed."

"What does Edie say about it?"

"She hasn't answered my calls. Right now, she's in the middle of a personal problem."

"To hell with her personal problem," he said, standing and tucking in his shirt. "You've got one of those yourself. Your creditors won't wait."

The doorbell rang. When Mary Ellen looked out the window, she saw men from the electronics company standing on her doorstep, ready to repossess her equipment. Tears of frustration suddenly blurred her vision. "Damn. Double damn."

Greg must have known immediately what was happening. He walked to the door and, without ceremony, asked how much was owed.

One young man looked down at his clipboard and gave the amount. But when he looked back up, his gaze was distant. "Cash or money order only."

"Can you wait fifteen minutes?" Greg asked, pulling out his keys. "There's a bank at the end of the street. I'll get a cashier's check there."

"Yes, sir."

"Greg, no!" Mary protested, reaching for his arm.

Greg didn't waste time; he was already halfway to the car. "Wait here. I'll be right back."

Mary gave a weak smile and shrugged at the two young men. She felt so embarrassed, but short of wishing the sidewalk would swallow her up, there was nothing she could do. Instead, she gestured toward the door.

"Please, come in. We might as well wait in comfort." Besides, maybe the neighbors wouldn't notice and wonder what was going on.

The electronics men were almost as uncomfortable as she was. They sat stiffly in the reception area for the next ten minutes until Greg walked in and handed them a cashier's check for just over two thousand dollars. In fifteen seconds, the men were gone, and Mary stood awkwardly in front of Greg, not sure whether to yell at him or thank him profusely. The creditors might have left, but she was still embarrassed.

Greg solved it all. Placing his hands on her shoulders, he spoke quietly. "Darlin', don't say a word. We'll work this out, taking the money out of a second check. Let me look into things, okay?"

Within minutes he was on the phone with his secretary, giving orders and getting things done. Mary watched quietly, and for the first time realized what it was like to have a man who was on her side and in charge.

She'd never been taken care of before and it brought a lot of mixed feelings to the fore. But the most prevalent one right now was sheer and utter relief....

10

EDIE ARRIVED AT MARY'S around eight o'clock that night, looking even more haggard than Greg had looked earlier, if that was possible. Mary was finishing up the cabinet trim in the kitchen before replacing the doors, hoping this would be the last night for that particular chore. She was sick of it.

As angry as Mary was with her secretary, Edie was a welcome diversion. "Explain what happened, Edie. What did you do with the check?"

Edie looked blankly at her boss. "Check? I cashed it. Both of them."

Mary almost dropped her paintbrush. "What 'both of them' are you talking about? We only received one."

Frowning, Edie wearily plopped in a straight-backed chair. "Are you talking about my pay and bonus check?"

"No." Mary barely held on to her patience. "I'm discussing the Torrance check."

Edie's eyes grew wide with understanding. "I didn't do anything with it except make out the deposit slip. I thought you took care of it!"

Panic gripped Mary's stomach. "Where did you last see it?"

"On your desk."

Mary mentally rifled through a hundred papers she'd seen in the past week. She'd swear there hadn't been a check among them. "Where?"

"I put it in the In basket."

Mary dropped her paintbrush and almost ran into her office. Once there, she plowed through the untouched paperwork in her basket. Then she saw it: it was the bottom item. Carefully attached to it by two paper clips was the deposit slip—all filled out and ready for the bank.

"Oh, my God," she muttered. "I've gone through a month of hell in a week, and it was here all the time."

Edie followed her into the office. "I'm sorry," she said, still looking slightly confused. "I know work's been hectic, but I had no idea you hadn't deposited it."

"We discussed who would go to the bank, but I thought we decided you would go." Mary continued to stare at the check. "It was here all the time! They came to repossess my audio equipment today and Greg Torrance got a cashier's check to bail me out."

"Oh, dear heavens," Edie gasped, leaning against the wall. "I had no idea. I thought I told you where it was before I left last week. It's my fault. I'm so sorry."

Mary Ellen glanced at her watch. It was too late to go to the bank and explain today. She'd do that in the morning. But right now she had a few

other problems to work out. She smoothed out
the check and placed it squarely in the center of
her desktop. Then she looked long and hard at
her secretary. "Okay, let's start again. What's going on?"

Edie's eyes teared up, her expression so sad
that Mary wanted to hug her, but thought better
of it. Sitting down on the love seat she'd shared
with Greg earlier that day, she patted the cushion
beside her. "Come on. Let's talk."

"Grant's still in jail, Mary," Edie said quietly,
curling her legs underneath her and leaning into
the cushions. "I didn't know it, but he had another ticket last year for drinking and driving.
They gave him probation and he never told me.
But I should have known. I should have seen the
signs." She closed her eyes for a moment and
leaned her head against the couch. "Good grief,
looking back, they were like bright red flags
waving in a stiff breeze! After getting the ticket
and taking this mandatory class about the problem, he stopped drinking. I didn't know the
cause of it, but I was thrilled. Then he slowly
started up again." Edie pushed her hair away
from her face. "One day I realized he was drinking more than ever. And when he drinks more
than one or two, he gets angry at everything. He
picks on me—and then argues with the kids.
When I said something about it one morning, he
stated that he was only having an occasional beer
in the evening. No big deal, he said. After all, he
was drinking them at home, not on the road or in

some sleazy bar. And I wanted to believe, so I did. I guess I ignored the truth, hoping the problem would go away."

"But it didn't," Mary Ellen prompted.

Edie shook her head. "No, it didn't. I found out he was keeping a case of beer on ice in a cooler in the garage." She clenched her hands in her lap. "I couldn't deny the problem anymore. When I confronted him, he got angry, cursed me out and drove off. That was about eight-thirty, five nights ago. Four o'clock in the morning, I got a call that he'd been arrested. It's been a nightmare ever since."

Mary's heart went out to her friend. She reached over and grasped Edie's hands. "Has he always drunk like that?"

Edie's shoulders drooped. "No. At least not lately. When we were first married, I think he fought the idea of growing up and being the man in the household. It scared the hell out of him," she said, giving a timorous grin. "But he finally stopped running with the boys and took more and more of the responsibilities of a man and a new father. We've been together for a long time, and this is the first time I've seen him revert back to that life-style."

"What do you think caused it?"

"I don't know." Edie closed her eyes and swallowed hard. "All I know is that there isn't enough money to get him out. The attorney's fees ate all my bonus and most of my paycheck, but we still don't have the money for bail. I'm so damn scared that his boss will fire him. Grant called in and said he needed some vacation time to visit a sick relative, but if they find out differently…"

"How much more do you need?"

Edie named almost the same amount Greg had just paid for Mary Ellen to keep her equipment. But it didn't take a minute for her to decide what needed to be done. "Look," she said, standing and going to the desk. She grabbed her checkbook and began writing. "Take this to the bondsman and see if he'll hold it until tomorrow, when I go to the bank and explain what happened. By that time, they'll let the funds skate through, I'm sure." She tore off the check and held it out to an astonished Edie. "But that means you'll have to come back to work ASAP." Mary grinned. "We'll have to finish the Torrance deal quickly so I can get the money back. Okay?"

Edie stood up, her expression one of wonder and awe as she reached for the check. She stared at it for a long moment. "You'd do this for me?" she finally asked, her voice barely a croak.

Mary Ellen looked surprised. "Of course! Why wouldn't I? As long as I have it, I can share it with my friend."

Edie's eyes brimmed with tears. Immediately, Mary enveloped her shaking shoulders in a hug. The two women stood together, sharing the heartache over a loved one, the hurt of deception and the comfort of help in a time of trouble.

And they clung together because they needed

the human contact with someone who cared, someone who suffered and understood....

Over a cup of tea they finally sat and talked for another hour, sharing hopes and dreams and occasional sadness, as only good friends could do. At last, Edie sighed and wiped her eyes. She looked down at her feet, embarrassed. "Thanks, Mary. I won't forget this."

"Thanks, Edie." Mary Ellen grinned. "Neither will I."

"I'll pay you back."

"Yes, I know."

Edie finally looked up. "I'm supposed to be the older one, your mother figure," she said, her voice still hoarse from emotion.

"Not tonight," Mary corrected, still grinning. "You can do that when I need motherly advice again."

"Oh, good. I have a job *and* my status to maintain. Thanks."

"Great. Now get out of here and I'll see you day after tomorrow. But I want a full report on any changes."

Just then the clock struck midnight, and Edie glanced at her watch for confirmation. "I really have got to go," she said tiredly. "I've got a bondsman to meet in the early a.m. and a boss who's obviously lost her mind enough and needs my help."

"Amen to both," Mary Ellen said, stretching her arms above her head. "I've got a bank appointment and a film to organize."

Edie gave her one more quick hug. "Thanks again, boss. If all goes well, I'll see you day after tomorrow."

As Edie drove off, Mary Ellen watched from the window until the headlights disappeared. Then she locked the doors and headed upstairs. It was late, she hadn't heard from Greg and she was dead tired.

"To hell with everyone. I'm going to sleep," she muttered, turning out the last light and stripping quickly before diving under the covers and closing her eyes. She was asleep immediately.

A BELL KEPT RINGING. Mary covered her head to block out the sound.

Several minutes later, the ringing began again. She still ignored it.

By the third time, she was half-awake, but when she finally picked up the offending phone, the caller had hung up.

Glancing at the clock gave Mary Ellen a start. It was a little after eight in the morning. She had many things to do today, and not enough time to do them!

After she'd showered and dressed, she was ready to face the answering machine downstairs. Everyone else had been busy this morning, judging from the messages lined up and waiting.

"Hi, dear. This is Edie, on my way to the bondsman. I'll let you know the results. Take care and have a successful day. I'll see you tomorrow—I hope."

Click. Beep.

"Hello, Ms. Gallagher. This is your bank and we need you to call us this morning. It is of the utmost urgency. We already tried your cell phone and beeper with no results. My name is Becky and I'll be here all day."

Click. Beep.

Four more messages were from irritated creditors, and then Greg's voice filled the room. "Hello, beautiful. Jason is still in the hospital but doing very well. I think he'll be out by this weekend. I'll call you sometime soon. I miss you."

It might have been the heightened emotions left over from last night. It might have been the stress of the past five days. It might have been the loneliness for Greg and the emptiness she felt without him. All she knew was that she'd had enough of being stoic and strong and capable. She was tired of the whole damn struggle.

No one was around. No one could see her. No one cared.

Mary Ellen Gallagher sat down and bawled.

She cried and cried, hiccuping over every error she'd ever made, over every time she'd wanted to lean on someone and there'd been was no one around. She remembered every time she'd wanted her family and they'd been separated by too many miles to get together; every time she'd ever needed help and there'd been no one to call on.

But then her tumbled emotions changed. What began as feeling sorry for herself changed into longing and wishing she was with the one she loved. She wanted Greg to hold her and tell her that everything would be all right. It didn't matter whether or not it was true; she just wanted to hear it, and for a little while believe in that particular dream.

Whenever she thought she was through with tears, they would begin again, and it was over an hour before she trusted herself to go to the bank and not have a crying jag in front of one of the officers.

BY LATE AFTERNOON, Mary Ellen was back home. She dropped her purse in the foyer and walked into the kitchen. With careful precision, she poured herself a glass of wine.

That huge empty cavern in the pit of her heart was still empty, still sore, still ready to trigger tears. Only sheer willpower kept her from folding into a soggy, bawling mess on the couch.

The phone rang and she picked up the receiver.

"Hello, wonderful woman. How are you?"

Warmth shot through her, filling her with the first good feelings she'd experienced all day. "Hello there. I'm sorry I missed your call. How's Jason?"

"He'll be home tomorrow, thank goodness." There was a moment of hesitation. "I've got to attend a business dinner tonight. Will you be up to having a guest afterward?"

Her heart raced at the thought. "I'd love to. Are you sure *you'll* be up to it?"

"I'm sure." he said with certainty. "I'll be there around midnight, okay?"

When Greg hung up, Mary held on to the phone for just a moment longer. She had needed to hear his voice, his reassurance that all was well between them. She needed to know that she was important to him.

No matter how much of a feminist she was, how much she had done on her own or how much she was capable of doing, she wanted the man she loved to be there, too. It wasn't the same without Greg.

The photo layout she'd done for his manufacturing plant was going well. By late evening she'd set up the entire shoot, formed the plan of camera angles and basic lighting and knew she was ready to put her plan into action.

Tomorrow was Friday and Edie would be back, which meant Mary Ellen could start shooting the Torrance film and preparing for voice-over and editing. If she was lucky, she'd have the job completed in another two weeks. Not bad for the money. And who knew? If she got a few more breaks like the Torrance account, her goal of becoming the number one VHS film company in Houston could be within reach....

But goals weren't on her mind when she opened the door and saw Greg standing on her porch. The single yellow bulb burned planes and angles into his square-jawed face. His beloved face. He looked as tired and haggard as she'd ever seen him. And he seemed just as pleased to see her as she was to see him.

Without saying anything, he enfolded her in his arms and gave her a kiss she wouldn't soon forget. His mouth was strong and firm and knowing and needing, and he took everything she could give and gave as good as he got.

Too soon, he pulled away and rested his forehead against hers, his warm breath caressing her ear and the slope of her neck. "I missed you so much," he murmured.

"I missed you, too."

His entire being seemed weary. "As much as you can miss some inconsequential man in your life," he said.

Mary didn't answer. She wasn't sure what to say. His mood seemed at once needy and distant. But whatever happened, she couldn't tell him she was so in love with him that all she could think or do was wrapped up in him.

She served him a cup of coffee and they sat in the office and talked. He spoke about Jason, about work and its problems, and about Janet— how wonderfully she'd handled the situation. All situations. Any situation.

Janet was the saint, and Mary was the one listening.

When Greg and she went to bed, Mary Ellen took her time in the bathroom. She had bought a new, cream-colored shortie gown and was sure Greg would like it. But when she walked back in the room, it was dark. His head was turned toward the window, his eyes closed.

"Greg?" she whispered. "Greg?" she called just a little louder.

Mary leaned over and stared into his face. A small puff of air parted his lips. He was asleep.

With a grin and a feeling of resignation, she crawled into bed. Even though he was sleeping, he turned and cuddled next to her. His warm body molded to hers spoon-fashion and he kissed her nape, giving a low, satisfied moan. A few minutes later, she was fast asleep.

GREG AWOKE in the middle of the night. He was holding Mary Ellen, his heart thudding from a dream he'd had. He'd dreamed he'd lost her. She was running away from him as fast as she could and he was racing after her until he thought his heart would explode with the exertion. Fear and tension made his body break into a sweat.

Damn!

He loved her.

It was as plain as the pumps on his factory floor. It had probably been apparent to everyone else—including Mary Ellen—for ages.

He was madly, passionately in love with the tall, slender girl-woman curled next to him. Every muscle and fiber in his body called out to love her, honor her, protect her against all of life's evils. He didn't want to imagine living day to day without her presence. He couldn't face not hearing her voice two, three, a hundred times a day. It was inconceivable to him to be without her.

Aside from loving the way her luscious body curved to his so perfectly when they made love, there was so much more. He loved the way she smiled, the way she tilted her head when she was thinking, the way her eyes lit up with merriment. He loved watching her figure something out; whatever it was, she would frown, then the invisible wheels would start to crank, and she wouldn't let go until she had a solution or two or three.

There wasn't a damn thing he didn't love about her, and yet he hadn't realized that until this very moment.

And he didn't have a clue what to do about it.

Should he tell her? Ask her to marry him? Have her move in?

He was more afraid to bring up any of those solutions and be rejected than he'd been of getting his divorce.

He'd loved Janet—still did—but not like this. Janet was his friend. She'd always been just that, only he hadn't known it. Hell, until Mary Ellen, he hadn't had a clue about real love. But now he did. Now he knew the depth and breadth of emotions he'd always thought were saved for country songs and dramatic teenagers.

This woman was his life. His breath.

His heart.

His heartbeat slowed down. It was about time

he finally consciously admitted what he'd been feeling all this time.

He would propose.

He'd propose next week. He didn't know how or when, but he'd make time for them sometime soon. After Jason was home and all was well with his son.

Greg took a deep breath and closed his eyes. Now that that decision was out of the way, he could sleep. Still holding Mary Ellen close, he drifted into contented slumber.

MARY WORKED HARD all day at Greg's factory. He was in meetings and unable to join her or watch the filming, which in many ways made it easier for her. She didn't have to worry about him observing her work or to wonder what he was thinking about.

At first, she set up shot after shot, hoping to catch employees acting natural in their jobs instead of posing for the camera. But after three hours of trying, she finally gave up and went for the obvious solution.

Choosing several workers, she had them look up as she panned the camera in their direction. Each one smiled at the camera for a few seconds before getting back to work.

By the end of the day she was drained. She packed up her equipment and headed for home. Jason was being discharged from the hospital this afternoon, so she knew she wouldn't be seeing Greg.

Once home, she fixed herself a pot of tea. The kitchen painting was done; the rewiring was complete. Countertops were being done by professionals early next week and the floor tiles were in boxes by the back door. This room, the hardest so far, was almost finished.

Edie strolled in. "Hi, there, boss. I heard you drive up." She looked closer, frowning. "Are you okay? You look like you've gone through a wringer somewhere."

Mary poured herself a cup of tea. "I didn't realize you were still here. Is everything all right?'

"Don't change the subject," Edie ordered, a smile tilting her lips. "Thanks to you, everything's fine. How did the shoot go?"

"I feel good about it, but I'll know more when I look at the film."

Edie glanced down at the cup Mary held. "Was Greg there?"

"No. He had meetings, then had to pick up his son from the hospital."

"Are you two still an item?"

"Am I still seeing him? Yes." Mary could tell by the way Edie was acting that something had happened. "'Fess up. What's wrong?"

Edie hesitated for a full minute. Mary remained quiet, waiting, knowing it was something she didn't want to hear. Something she needed to know but wouldn't like....

"The only reason I'm showing you this is because I don't want you hurt again. You deserve so much more than this...."

"Show me."

Edie placed a folded newspaper on the table. Big and bold, a photo of Greg and Janet smiled up at her, their arms around each other. Even before Edie spoke, Mary Ellen knew what the article said.

"Greg was with his ex-wife at some charity banquet last night," Edie murmured. "The news is that they were reconciling and wedding bells would be heard real soon."

For a full minute, Mary's heart stopped. When it started up again, it felt like lead. "That doesn't make it so," she stated softly.

"Only they would know that, Mary," Edie said, her tone gentle but firm. "I wanted you to see this just in case he's really a rat."

Mary barely heard Edie. She'd given her heart to a man who didn't love her in return. Greg had only needed her to fill the void while he patiently waited for his wife to come to her senses. Humiliation filled her soul. The man she loved didn't love her, but had gone back to his ex-wife. It was happening all over again.

Mary Ellen felt used. Dirty. Her soul ached with the realization of how low he'd stooped, using her as he had. But something inside reminded her that she had had a hand in it, too. Despite the protests from him and his ex-wife, she'd known from the beginning that he was still in love with Janet. Mary Ellen decided to play the game with the big boys anyway, thinking that it wouldn't hurt to climb into bed with him as long as she remembered the rules: no commitments, only fun.

What a laugh. She might have known the rules, but she hadn't obeyed them. She'd been left for another woman. The first woman.

Again.

She blinked back the tears, letting anger with herself dry them up. "May the best woman win," she said to no one in particular. Lifting her cup in the air, she saluted Edie. Then she sipped the hot brew. But she couldn't carry the casual attitude any further. Instead, she sat down and stared into her tea.

"Mary, I'm so sorry. I feel as if I started this romance, and I shouldn't have."

"You didn't. I did this all on my own, Edie."

"I know, but I encouraged it. I thought he was on the level, not the kind of louse that would bed one woman while in love with another."

Mary gave a halfhearted smile. "It's not your fault. I seem to draw this kind of rat. It must be my karma." She took another drink of tea, slugging it down as if it were whiskey and glad it wasn't or she'd be drunk. "I couldn't have been convinced to have this relationship if I hadn't wanted it."

"I know, but…" Edie began, only to realize by the look on Mary's face that she didn't want to hear any more about it. "I'll finish up the paperwork," she said, leaving the room.

Mary finally found the nerve to pick up the paper and stare down at the photo. It was on the front page of the life-style section, its full blazing color almost blinding her eyes—and tearing her heart apart. Greg stood with his arm around Janet, his head tilted toward her, a smile on his lips. Janet was beaming at the camera as if she was exactly where and with whom she wanted to be. The headline read Biggest Charity Draw Ever. The rest of the article explained how Janet and Greg had co-chaired the charity ball, and why they'd chosen a children's cause. It also intimated that they would always work together, for the sake of "their" children, to insure there would be money available for research. The end of the article stated that they had been divorced, but were changing their minds as they spoke. Apparently, the marriage was on again.

Apparently.

The private telephone line rang, but Mary ignored it. The business line rang and Edie picked it up. She came to the kitchen door, her eyes filled with concern. "It's Greg. He says he needs to talk to you."

Mary looked up, her eyes remote. "Sure. Why not?"

Edie picked up the cordless phone and handed it to her. Mary greeted him cooly.

"Mary? Is everything all right?"

"Fine. Why?"

"I don't know. You sound different."

"Everything's fine. What can I do for you?" She kept her tone distant, businesslike. She couldn't get emotional now, not if she was going to make it through their phone conversation.

"I promised Jason I'd spend the evening with him, but let's go out to eat tomorrow night. Just the two of us."

"I'm sorry," she said calmly. "I've already made plans. In fact, I've got plans for the rest of the next two weeks."

There was a long, tension-filled silence before Greg spoke again. "You saw the article."

"What article?"

"Don't play games, Mary." His voice was downright belligerent. "You saw the article in the paper and believed the stupid journalist who wrote it, didn't you?"

"I have plans." Her voice was calm and distant, firm and quiet—a deadly combination. "They have to do with work. I just don't have time to spend on anything but my career—I've put off too many things for too long."

"You're running."

"Yes. Right toward my goals."

"Don't snow me, Mary. We're a pair, you and me, and we need to be together."

"You're already part of a pair. I'll have your video finished in the next two weeks and I'll get it to you. Until then, I've got enough work to keep me busy twenty hours a day for the next month or more. Please excuse me. I have to go now."

"I thought you understood that the one thing I need from you is trust—"

He was still speaking as she quietly pushed the button and disconnected the line.

Then she sat and stared at the cabinets again, her mind a blank. Her heart thudding in her chest told her she was alive. Otherwise she might not have known.

11

GREG'S ABSENCE from her life caused a whirling frenzy in Mary Ellen's mind and body every waking hour. As long as she was busy, she didn't have to think. When she stopped moving, bitter reality assailed her—so she just kept on working.

She worked steadily from six o'clock in the morning to after midnight every night. She worked on every aspect of her business, while also completing whatever house repairs she was capable of handling herself.

Greg called every day, leaving messages. First he asked her to call. Then he told her to call. Then he demanded she call. Although Jason was home from the hospital, he was still in bed, and Greg and Janet were taking turns going to work so the other could stay with him.

By the third week, Mary was out of the office every day, working the field until she was thinner than she'd ever been and twice as nervous. Greg came by twice, both times sitting with Edie and waiting. To no avail. Three times Mary Ellen ate at Edie's, then, too tired to make it home, spent the night there.

In the home-renovation area, only one thing was completely out of her hands. The wiring that

Greg had been working on was almost—but not quite—complete. She'd have to wait until she finished a few more film projects and got paid before she would be able to complete the work she wanted done. It would just take a little time, that was all.

But in the back of her mind was the image of Greg making love to her, whispering in her ear how wonderful, sweet and sexy she was. Greg holding her in the dark of night until she fell asleep. She saw the laughter in his hazel eyes, the rumpled look of his hair when he was lost in thought and ran his hand through it.

She tried to chase away those images quickly, but it seldom worked. Within seconds, tears would blur her vision and a frog would close her throat. A terrible heaviness encompassed her heart.

She worked herself into the ground, knowing what she was doing and yet ignoring it. She knew Edie was watching her, but they both kept silent on the subject.

Two weeks later, Edie had hit her limit of patience and walked determinedly into the sound room with a resolute glint in her eyes. "We've got to talk."

Mary sat at the console, headphones perched on her head, but not covering her ears enough to block out Edie's words. She was dubbing the narration on a film for a huge family reunion. "Can't talk now," she said, using her headphones as a shield.

But Edie knew better. She reached over and punched the Stop button, then pulled the plug on the headphones. She stood with her hands on her hips.

Mary stared in surprise. She'd never seen Edie quite so adamant before.

Edie gave a tight, quick smile. "Now, I know you're gun-shy. And I know you don't and didn't deserve the nasty men in your life so far. And I know that someday you'll find the right man for you. But please don't settle for Mr. Wrong just because Mr. Right hasn't come along yet."

"Okay," Mary said softly.

"I know it seems as if Grant and I don't stand a chance in hell of making our marriage work, but you just might be wrong." She defended everything that had happened in her marriage in that sentence. "We're in counseling now, and so far it's working. But we had something special between us to begin with. You never did with Joe— not that it would have mattered, because he's the rear end of a horse, anyway."

Mary Ellen wondered where this was going or if Edie just needed someone to talk to and this was the spillover. "Okay."

"So, I'm here for you. No matter what. And if you're lonely, you can call on me. We can go to the movies or walking in the park, or shopping, or—"

Mary Ellen had to stop her. This had gone far enough. "Edie, I don't go shopping or to the movies and neither do you. So, what's this about?''

Edie looked impatient, as if Mary hadn't heard what she'd said. "Joe is on the porch, waiting to see you. I hope it's hot as hell out there.''

Mary carefully slipped off her headphones and stood, straightening her T-shirt. "Do I look good?'' she asked, smoothing back her midnight black hair. She'd just washed it this morning and it hung straight and shiny.

Edie was incredulous. "You're not trying to impress *him*, are you?''

Mary grinned mischievously. "No. I just want him to eat his heart out when he sees what he lost.''

Edie laughed, her expression reflecting her relief. "You could have been playing in the mud and he'd eat his heart out. He's a loser looking for a winner.''

"Thanks!'' Mary gave Edie a quick hug. "Wish *this* winner good luck.''

She strode to the front door, only to stop just before opening it. She took a deep breath and ordered her pulse to calm down. This was hard. On the other side of the door was the man she'd thought she loved enough to marry. She'd been wrong. She hadn't really loved Joe any more than he'd loved her. It had been her pride that was hurt, her ego that was torn to shreds. Joe hadn't crushed her heart.

Greg had done that.

Joe didn't stand a chance against her resolve to

have nothing more to do with him. But just before she stepped outside, she bit her lips and pinched her cheeks, then smoothed her already smooth hair into place and put on a disinterested look.

Joe stood casually by the porch railing, staring at the new grouping of pink and purple petunias down below that Mary had planted less than three days ago. From the way he was staring, as if in a pose, Mary knew he'd heard her approach and decided to ignore her until he knew how she'd react.

"Hi."

He looked up, feigning surprise, then allowed a broad smile to spread across his handsome face. "Hello, beautiful."

She ignored his charm, which was as fake as a used-car salesman's. "What brings you here, Joe? I thought we said everything there was to say."

"Not by a long shot." He came toward her. "I missed you."

Mary tilted her head and looked up at him, curiosity in her gaze. "Did you really? Then why did you leave?"

He had the grace to blush. "Because I didn't know what I was doing. Lisa was so, well…I'll explain later."

"Was she more beautiful? More dutiful? More sexy? Help me out here. Give me a clue, Joe."

"She just didn't care as much as I thought she did. That's all. She just plain didn't care." He focused on Mary. "And I didn't, either, but I didn't realize it until it was too late and I'd lost you."

"So you don't think she loved you?" Mary Ellen persisted.

"No, not really." He glanced at the window, and Mary realized that Edie was probably right behind the shutter. "Can we go somewhere else and talk? I'm not sure I like your secretary standing guard."

"Well," Mary said slowly, as if thinking it over. "You could come back this evening and take me out to dinner."

He snapped at the bait. "Great. What time?"

"In a couple of hours." She glanced at her watch. "Say, about seven o'clock?"

"I'll be back," he promised, placing his hands on her shoulders and giving a squeeze. "I promise."

"See you then," she said, wishing he would leave quickly so she could move ahead with the rest of the plan she had just formed.

He gave her a quick kiss on the forehead and turned to go down the stairs. Then he looked back at her. "You won't be sorry."

"I hope not, Joe. I hope not."

When she stepped inside the house, Edie was waiting, her expression nothing less than incredulous. "Why in heaven would you want to go out with that piece of worthless slime?" she demanded.

"Because I have this screwball feeling that he really loves her and should be with her. But he's just not smart enough to know what to do about it.''

Edie looked dumbfounded. "What?"

"Look, I know how stupid the man is, but everyone deserves his dreams. Joe's dream was to have a wife and family and be the father everyone looked up to for a job well done. If he grows up enough, he just might make it with Lisa.''

"And who gives a damn whether he makes it or not?'' Edie argued. "He's still the same slime-ball who left you at the altar just hours before the wedding.''

"I know, I know," she said. "But a girl's gotta do what a girl's gotta do.''

"Yeah," Edie muttered as she grabbed her purse to head for home. "Like go insane.''

But she still stopped to give Mary a hug before she left.

Mary dressed carefully. For the first time since Joe had walked out on her, she was pleasantly looking forward to seeing him. She made several phone calls, setting up what she hoped was going to be a happy ending.

When Joe arrived all decked out in a new gray suit, she was wearing a bright red dress and carefully prepared makeup, and her hair was smoothly swept up. She felt like a sexy, heart-breaking "other woman" for a change, instead of one who'd been dumped and left behind. And that feeling put an extra little swing in her walk.

That same thought was echoed in Joe's eyes.

"You look fantastic," he said, his gaze as appreciative as his words.

"Thank you. Did you have some special place in mind?" she asked.

"Not really. I thought we'd go to that new Italian restaurant that just opened."

Mary pouted prettily—at least she tried to. "Do you mind if we go to the Post Oak Grill and grab a bite? I've got a yen for one of their dishes."

Joe hesitated for just a minute before placing a smile on his face and going into his genial, easygoing act. "Of course not. Whatever you like," he said.

He hadn't changed at all. He still did whatever he could to please the woman in his life, including spending too much money on dinner. But sooner or later resentment grew until he blew up from accumulated anger, and no one would know what caused the explosion—including himself.

Once they were seated at the restaurant, Joe leaned forward. "Mary Ellen, you look fabulous."

"Thank you," she said with the sexiest smile she could manage. "But who you really want to be with tonight is your wife. Not me, Joe."

He stiffened. "That's not true."

Mary looked over toward the door. For the first time in three years, she and the woman she'd thought was her rival stared at each other. Mary Ellen gave a small nod of acknowledgment, then looked at Joe.

With his wife at the entrance of the restaurant, she had to speak quickly. "You might not know it, but you love Lisa. You wouldn't have left me for her if you didn't. So listen hard and quick, Joe. I had a long talk with her today, and she loves you very much. In fact, she's going to be sitting here in a few minutes, and you'd better be smart enough to make up with her. Your dreams are just as important as anyone else's, but you'd better learn to voice your own feelings as you feel them, or others will never know what you need until it's too late. And turnabout is fair play. When she has a gripe, my man, she's letting you know and you're brushing it off. Shame on you. If you want happiness, you've got to work for it. God doesn't just drop it in your lap."

Joe sat staring at her as if she were an alien from outer space.

Mary Ellen smiled. "Now, my dear Joe, I'm being as kind as I can. In return you can name your first child after me. So sit here and tell your wife what you would have told me about her, except use a little discretion—and truth. You'll be amazed at how your dreams can come true if you work on them." She gave him a pointed look. "And that's my exit line." She stood and reached for her small red bag. "Good luck."

Joe sat stiffly, watching her leave. But when his gaze found the blond woman standing uncertainly at the entrance, Mary knew she'd done the right thing.

"He loves you," Mary whispered as she passed her. "Good luck."

The young blonde bobbed her head, then took the first determined step toward Joe's table.

Mary decided she deserved a drink and walked to the bar, where she ordered a glass of wine and sat listening to the pianist. From her perch, Mary Ellen could just see Joe and Lisa in the bar mirror. Lisa was sitting quietly while Joe did some defensive talking.

It was funny how Mary could watch the two and hope for their success at making up without feeling bad about losing Joe. It had been another lifetime ago when she had thought she knew what love was. She'd been wrong then, but she knew love now. And the knowledge was as heartbreaking as anything she'd ever experienced.

"My God. My first business dinner in two weeks and the very person I need more than life itself is in the same restaurant. What do you think about the chances of it being a fluke?"

Greg stood by her side. She'd smelled the scent of his aftershave and had known it was him just an instant before he spoke. The hair on the back of her neck still stood on end. Her heart raced with excitement and anticipation and she tried to calm herself. Nothing had changed. He was still emotionally tied to his wife. "Do you usually trade dates with other women, or is this something new and savvy I haven't heard about?"

She continued to stare into her drink rather

than look at him. If she glanced into his eyes, her resolve would crumble and she'd be a goner. A loser in the game of life, as Edie would say. "It's none of your business."

Ignoring her tone of voice, Greg slid onto the stool next to her. "You're my business. I can't help it. I love you."

She stared straight ahead and sipped her wine, but her insides trembled mightily. She could dream all she wanted to, but that wouldn't make the words any more true than Joe's words had been. "Sure you do. I'm right up there with about four or five others."

"You're being unreasonable. Why? What are you so scared of, Mary?" Greg's voice was low, tense, angry. "A small boy who needs a father? That will never change as long as I'm alive or who I'm in love with. A company that needs my direction to keep it going? Since it didn't exist before I built it, I don't see how letting it go would prove anything except that I'm a nutcase. Or are you just too damn scared of love to give of yourself to anyone, especially me?"

Staring straight ahead, Mary remained silent. She couldn't answer, because she *was* afraid. Afraid he might be right and she might be wrong...

Someone called his name, and out of the corner of her eye she saw him wave the person away. Obviously he was with a group. The unexpected pain of seeing him was already too much to cope with. She didn't want to know where they were headed or where they'd come from. Or who he was with…

Greg tried to make a joke in the silence, but he sounded as frustrated as she felt. "If this is how you treat all the declarations of love you receive, Mary Ellen Gallagher, I understand how it might be a little daunting for the average male to continue with his courtship."

She didn't want to look at him, but she couldn't stop herself. Dressed impeccably in a dark blue suit and yellow tie, he was just as handsome as ever. His hazel eyes were just as intimate, as deep and abiding as in her dreams. But she knew better. The look he was now giving her was the same one he'd given his wife the night their son was ill. It was the look that had gotten him where he was. It said he cared, he worried and he was involved in her happiness. But it wasn't necessarily true.

"Talk to me, Mary."

The silence between them was not going to go away. Neither was Greg, at least not until he heard from her.

She said the first thing she could think of to deflect his attention from her. Nodding toward Joe's table, she murmured, "I just finagled Joe into talking to his wife. I called Lisa and asked her to meet us here. She's pregnant and he doesn't know it yet. Having a stay-at-home wife and a family was his dream."

"You're an unusual woman. Most would jab him between the eyes with a dull fork, but you give him the main course of his own private dreams."

"It wasn't easy, and I had to forgive a lot. But he belonged back home with his wife, not with me. Just like you. So, what I did was exactly the right thing." She took another sip of her drink and slipped off the stool. "Just like leaving now is the right thing to do."

"Ma'am, your tab," the bartender reminded her.

She smiled tightly. "Mr. Torrance is buying my drink and giving you a hefty tip."

She heard Greg give a low curse under his breath and knew she'd gotten to him. It was an insult—one he wouldn't soon forget.

Then she walked away, looking directly ahead of her. If she put one foot in front of the other, she'd get out this door and into a taxi; if luck was with her, she'd be home in less than twenty minutes. If she put one foot in front of the other she could save her pride; Greg wouldn't see her tears. If she put one foot in front of the other, she could get home and dream other dreams, leaving Greg out of the picture completely.

"Damn," she muttered as she reached the brass door and hailed the cab waiting yards away. She just needed to keep the tears away for twenty minutes more.

Her heart squeezed tightly. Her chest ached with anguish. Her bottom lip quivered as she gave her address. *Please let it wait until I reach home,* she prayed. But it wasn't to be. As she slipped into the back seat of the taxi and shut the door, the tears welled and a sob escaped her throat.

GREG WATCHED MARY ELLEN sashay out of the bar, and muttered a curse under his breath. It was obvious that she didn't feel a thing for him. Maybe she'd only gone to bed with him because she had nothing else to do. Maybe she…

He felt so damn frustrated! He'd wanted to hold her until she was convinced of his love. But because some punk in the next room had decided to wait until the last minute to break off their relationship, Greg was paying for it.

He'd called every day, sometimes twice a day. Hell, in the past two weeks, he'd talked more to Edie than he had to his own secretary! He and Edie had become good friends. She was encouraging, but knew that whatever it was Mary Ellen was working through, it was going to take time. Greg was ready to forget finesse, grab the recalcitrant woman and drag her out to his country cabin until she finally came to her senses. Of course, there was always the possibility that she might never want him again. That thought hurt too damn much; he wasn't even going to take a chance.

He stood up and strolled to the main entrance of the restaurant, spying Joe immediately. He was holding his wife's hand as if he'd just discovered gold. She was smiling sweetly, through tears.

At least some people had gotten what they wanted. But it sure as hell wasn't him.

He had to smile at the thought of the woman he loved, though.

She'd been a sexy little minx when she foisted her bar tab on him. She'd also been a cool customer when she told the story of what she'd done that night. What was he going to do to convince her that he was perfect for her—and she for him? Any problems they had they could work out, he was sure. Mary was so afraid of being hurt again that she was willing to go through life alone rather than take a chance. Yet she'd helped to restore the marriage of the very man who had emotionally burned her. Greg would have punched the bastard out.

Go figure.

So if she was brave enough to fight for someone else's happiness, why wasn't she brave enough to fight for her own? No answer came to mind. He doubted if Mary Ellen knew, either.

But he was certain of one thing. Everyone had a chink in their armor. Mary was no exception. There had to be a way to reach her. There had to be. And whatever it was, he would find it.

12

MARY WORKED FEVERISHLY to complete the Torrance assignment. Thanks to great preplanning and even greater good luck, she didn't have to return to his company for extra shots. From the beginning, she'd seen the whole project in her mind's eye, planned it out with still photos and then returned to shoot everything she needed and lots she didn't need. If luck was with her, she'd finish within the week.

She was proud of the work she'd done for Torrance. She'd followed the path of a pump from the sales order to completion and showed the caring and coping of several workers, who were so natural they could have been professional actors. In a stroke of genius, Mary had hired a female for the voice-over. Her tone was low, melodious and soothing, which somehow made magnetic pumps seem far more upbeat and interesting. And Mary Ellen would bet her paycheck that the men who stopped to look at the film would also hear everything this woman said. That coupled with the musical background was going to make this video one of her best. The score she'd chosen was one of the few pieces in her library that she would have to pay royalties on, but it was worth it. It gave the film a slick finishing touch. As soon as Mary received written permission to use the music, she'd include it in the credits and be finished.

Edie was still leaving work early, but felt so guilty about it she was even more efficient than usual. She and Grant were still going to a counselor, but if the bounce in Edie's step was any indication, Mary could safely place a bet that their marriage would work.

Edie entered the video room just as Mary was finishing up the film. She stood and watched the tail end in silence. "Wow. That's really good," she said. "Greg Torrance didn't pay you nearly enough."

Mary grinned widely. She had worked hard, but it had paid off. This was her best film yet. She felt pride in her work, and it felt good. "Thanks."

"Greg's secretary just called. She wants you to be at a press conference tomorrow morning at nine o'clock sharp. In their conference room. Bring your camera and document this time in history."

Mary's heartbeat raced. "Did she say what it was about?"

"Something about a public offering."

"And they want me to film the event?"

"Right. They thought it might work into the end of your Torrence video." Edie leaned against the door. "Then you can thumb your nose at him and say goodbye forever."

"Why not?"

"Except that you love him, don't you?"

Mary's smile disappeared. "Yes."

"And you want to live happily ever after."

"Which can never be."

"You know," Edie said thoughtfully, "last month I would have agreed with you."

Mary's brows rose. "But not now?"

"No, not now."

"Why?'

"Because it's too easy to run. It's not nearly as easy to stand and deliver. But when you run, you don't have a choice—you just plain lose. When you stand and deliver, you've got a fifty-fifty chance at happiness." Edie shrugged. "In my book, fifty-fifty makes more dreams come true than running away."

Edie knew just where to aim her sharpened arrows. Mary tried to deflect the barbs so they wouldn't pierce her. "Thank you for your philosophy lesson. I will keep it in mind, but I won't act on it. Now, get out of here and go play Pollyanna with your husband."

"See you early in the morning," Edie promised, not at all upset that her friend and boss had sloughed off her advice. "I'll be the secretary who brings you a banana and a glass of orange juice to fortify yourself before leaving for the big, bad conference."

Mary thought she'd brushed off Edie's words, but all evening long they haunted her. She had cut and run, but it was justified. She loved Greg but she didn't want to be hurt ever again.

That sounded sane, didn't it? Of course it did.

That night she fell asleep curled in the fetal position. But her dreams allowed her to stretch and grow and feel the light of love in her soul as if she was sunbathing. In her dreams, she was happy and contented, loved and treasured—all the things she'd always wanted, but hadn't had the nerve to believe in. She was flying over rooftops holding a package she didn't—couldn't—let go of. She didn't look down to see what it was. Instead she cradled it in her arms and enjoyed the scenery.

Even while she dreamed, she knew the sadness of present reality lay just beyond her dream world.

GREG LOOKED AT EASE and relaxed as he stood at the podium, a genuine smile on his face as he gazed around the large corporate boardroom. Half a dozen reporters and two TV cameras held command stations. About two dozen business associates and a few close friends milled around, chatting as if it was a social tea.

Janet stood by Greg's side, her smile as bright as the morning sun pouring through the windows. Another man stood a few feet away on her other side, looking awkward and clearly out of his element. Behind him were several other men and women. Mary Ellen surmised they were all members of the board of directors.

Young Jason stood with his hand in Janet's as she spoke to him in a low voice. He pulled a face that made Mary smile, then walked over to a stranger by the wall. Obviously he was eyeing another sweet roll on the sideboard, where coffee, tea and sweets were available for the press and guests.

Mary Ellen stood at the back of the room and set up her camera, ready for the announcement. She told herself that this was no different than filming any other event, but it didn't quite work. This time Greg was watching and that made a big difference. Her palms were wet, her ears rang and her heartbeat raced faster than a winning greyhound. Every time Greg looked her way, she felt her stomach drop.

But she gritted her teeth and promised herself that she would get through this ordeal if it was the last thing she did. Right this minute, it felt as if it *would* be the last thing....

Greg's voice broke into her thoughts. She flipped the On switch and turned to watch. "The Board of Torrance Corporation wants to thank you all for being here this morning. This announcement won't take long. But it is important, at least for the growth of our company in this community.

"As of seven a.m. next Monday, our company stock, now private, will be publicly traded over the New York Stock Exchange." There was a round of applause. "We're very proud of our growth and accomplishments these past ten years...." Greg went on to explain those accomplishments, many of which Mary Ellen had been aware of when she began the video. In fact, she'd highlighted several of them in the film.

Members of the board of directors beamed out at the audience. Everyone except the tall, silent man standing with Jason seemed thrilled with today's news.

The business reporters began asking questions, and Greg had all the answers. After fifteen minutes or so, he called a halt. "Please feel free to send us any questions that might not have been answered. But that's it for now."

The reporters were the first to leave the room. As the last ones straggled out, friends and business associates once more gave a round of applause to Greg and Janet. Voices blurred together in a cacophony resembling a cocktail party more than a breakfast.

After a few more minutes, Mary began packing up her gear. But Greg's voice cut through her automatic actions.

"We have one more announcement that might interest you all. The president of Torrance Corporation, Janet Torrance, has another piece of good news. She is marrying Dr. Tom Hendricks this coming June. We wish her and Tom the best of luck. It's not easy being married to a top-notch mechanical engineer whose company has just gone public."

There was more applause, and congratulations rang across the room. Everyone crowded up to the podium.

Mary stood quietly, her emotions churning.

She tried to make sense of it all, but her thoughts were so scattered she couldn't seem to focus. What did it all mean? Why wasn't Greg devastated? Even Jason was smiling.

Could she have been so very wrong about Greg and Janet's relationship? They had been so close, so intimate. She'd been so sure that they needed and secretly wanted to be together. In fact, she had bet her own happiness on being right.

Even Janet's plans to marry hadn't elicited a surprised response from anyone except Mary Ellen. If the response was to be believed, this was just a formal announcement. From the small talk she overheard, the group had apparently expected this action.

Greg's secretary entered the room from the side door and whispered something to him. He spoke to Janet and she nodded solemnly, taking her son's hand.

Greg turned back to the audience. "Thank you, ladies and gentlemen. Please continue to enjoy breakfast. Business calls," he said, and left quickly.

Mary's hands shook as she put her equipment away. She didn't know if there was a cure for love, and she wasn't even sure she wanted to find it unless it meant an end to this upheaval in her heart.

Her gaze darted to the man beside Janet, and she suddenly recognized him from the restaurant a month or so ago where she and Janet had met in the ladies' room. He'd seemed nice then, and Janet truly seemed to be in love.

As quickly as she could, Mary picked up her equipment and left by the side door, hurrying down the hall as if a herd of buffalo was after her.

For the next two days, she told herself that she couldn't handle the pressure of loving Greg and losing him. Not again. Then it dawned on her that she'd already lost him—and she'd done it all by herself. She'd kicked him out before he could leave her for someone else.

"Smooth move," she muttered under her breath that evening before going to bed. Without Greg in her life, she had nothing. Sure, she owned a business that was flourishing, she had money in the bank and creativity to spare. But she had no one who loved her, no one to share her success with.

Tears flowed every night. Determination faltered more every day. Mary Ellen had to admit to herself that by pulling away from Greg, she'd shot herself in the foot. Correction—in the heart.

Now she had to stop crying and decide what to do about it.

Unable to face him, she sent the completed Torrance video by courier. She was embarrassed, angry with herself and, most of all, full of longing for Greg, but she didn't know how to tell him so. She felt childish and awkward and confused.

There had to be a way to explain that she wanted back into his life. There had to be....

Mary dreamed that night that she was soaring

over rooftops with a treasured package in her arms—the same one as before. Greg was flying beside her. She wasn't sure, but she thought he wanted to take her package and she was afraid he'd drop it.

The next morning, she told Edie about the dream.

"When I took that course in dream interpretation, I found out that dreams are more simple than we like to believe. We mortals have a tendency to make things more complicated than they are." Edie looked thoughtful. "It sounds like you're carrying a child you want to keep safe and treasure, and he wants to share the burden, but you won't let him," she said.

Mary's eyes widened. She *had* been thinking about a child lately. She knew what Greg and Janet's child looked like, but she couldn't help wondering what Greg and *her* child would look like. Boy or girl? Tall or short? Blond or raven haired? Hazel or brown eyed?

"You think so?" she asked hopefully. The idea of a child thrilled her. She'd always dreamed of having both career and family. To have a child with Greg would be her most precious dream come true....

"I'd say so. But of course, you know best," Edie said softly.

After that conversation, Mary Ellen finally found the nerve to leave a message for Greg with his secretary. She asked that he call her when he had a chance. She prayed she hadn't made him so angry that he wouldn't consider trying once more.

She had no choice but to wait and hope it wasn't too late.

WHEN GREG RECEIVED Mary Ellen's message, he reached for the phone. Even though he was in a New York hotel room, he wanted to return her call right away. But another thought came fast on the heels of the first. What if she didn't want to talk to him? What if she just wanted to receive her final check? What if it was nothing but a business call?

Suddenly, the big, bad CEO of his own company was scared. He didn't have the nerve to call and hear about business. He didn't want to be rejected again.

He decided to wait until morning and talk to Edie first. She seemed to have a better handle on Mary Ellen than he did. Maybe she even had an idea or two that might help him. It would be easier to sell Edie on why he was good for her boss than to have one minute of shop talk with Mary....

That night, Greg stared at the city lights a long time before climbing into his lonely hotel bed. And when he did, he dreamed of flying....

Not only did Greg remember the dream, but he discussed it with Edie the next day.

"...And Mary was holding this bundle and wouldn't let me help," he said, as stunned that he was telling Edie about his dream as he was that he'd remembered it at all.

"Mmm," Edie said thoughtfully. "You know, dreams are easier to interpret than we realize. From the class I took, I would say that Mary is afraid of losing her identity, and she's afraid you'll take it from her. She needs your reassurance that you love her and she can have it all."

"You're right," he stated, deciding immediately that he had to try one more time to talk Mary into giving him a chance. "Edie, don't tell her. I'll be there late tonight. It's time Mary Ellen and I talked." It was both a promise and a threat.

"Okay, if you're sure that's what you want," Edie said, but she couldn't keep the glee out of her voice.

"I know what I want, all right." His own voice was grim. "And it's Mary Ellen Gallagher."

That certainly carried him all the way up to her door at midnight.

Mary sent a prayer of thanks heavenward as she watched him step out of the car and walk up to her house, just as Edie told her he would.

His knock was strong. Determined.

And when she opened the door, he stepped inside and wrapped his arms around her slim body as if he would never let her go. Ever. "You're mine and I'm yours. You can do whatever you like, I don't give a damn. You can have three full-time careers, travel to the moon and back or stay home and sit on your thumbs—I don't care. But when the day is done, you come into *my* arms and sleep with *my* body next to you. Understand?''

She covered his mouth with her fingers. ''Wait. I have to say this.'' She took a deep breath and continued in a rush. ''This is all my fault. My pride wouldn't let me tell you I'd made a mistake in judging you, and by the time I realized it, I thought you wouldn't get my message and then you wouldn't call and then I'd be so sick with love for you I'd never be able to function as an independent woman ever again. But the truth of it is that I love you with all my heart and I want to spend the rest of my life with you. I want to work together for a relationship that dreams are built on.''

Before she could say any more, Greg gave a deep laugh and captured her mouth, claiming her with a kiss that heated her all the way down to her toes. Her breath was stolen, her body flushed with the delicious taste of passion. And she was renewed with the realization of his love.

She pulled away, her hand cupping the side of his jaw. Her eyes were wide, sparkling with tears of joy. ''And if I wanted to stay home and raise children?''

''Great. I don't care, as long as you don't exclude me. They'll be my children, too, you know.'' He kissed her forehead, her temple, her cheek, his arms holding her as if she was a dream about to disappear into thin air.

''And if I wanted a career?''

"I don't care, as long as you don't exclude me. I have a career, too."

She felt warm and contented. "I love you." Her voice was soft. She outlined his mouth, circled his jaw and smiled. But there was still that small niggle of doubt. She had tried to cancel it out, stamp it to death, but it was there just the same. "And you're sure you really want me?"

Greg heaved a heavy sigh. "I'm answering this one more time, then never again, Mary Ellen. You'll just have to accept it as my answer."

"I promise."

"Janet and I are co-parents and business partners. That's all. If we had wanted to be more, we would have stayed together. We didn't. We're not."

"Thank you," Mary said softly. She knew it was time to trust again, but it was good to hear the words that erased her doubt just one more time.

"You know, people have been marrying and divorcing for years, but they don't always walk away before the ceremony. I won't, either. Surprisingly, even in divorce, there are lots of people who still remain civil to each other. It means two people are trying to salvage what they can to make a successful parenting team. That should be in my favor, not held against me."

"But—"

"No buts. I love you so much I ache with the thought of you leaving my arms, let alone leaving the room. However, I won't be accused of following in the footsteps of someone else who did you wrong. Either love me with trust in your heart or leave me now, before I lose my mind." His gaze was direct. Demanding. "Make your choice, Mary Ellen."

She stared into hazel eyes that seemed to hold the blue of the universe and the green of the ocean depths—and she felt a freedom she'd never felt before. She'd have doubts again, she was sure. But she would learn to deal with them until they disappeared. And they would disappear as she grew older and wiser. "Look how far I've come already," she said. "I chose you. I love you."

"I love you, too, Mary Ellen soon-to-be Torrance." His voice was husky with desire. "And I won't take no for an answer. Be my wife."

She smiled at the orders that rolled off his tongue. It didn't rankle her, it made her feel protected. The truth was she knew he was just as anxious about her answer as she had been about him. But now she could say what was in her heart. "I'm keeping Gallagher, Greg. My business was a success with that name, and I want to keep it."

Greg took a deep breath. "Fine. If that's what you want. I don't care as long as we're married."

She smiled. "I wouldn't have it any other way."

He kissed the tip of her nose. "Good. And right now, my darling, all I want to do is make love to you until one or both of us can't lift a finger."

Mary took his hand in hers and led him toward the staircase. "I happen to have a little kit upstairs that may help," she said, leading the way.

"And just where did you get that?" he asked. "Not that I need any help." But he continued to follow on her heels.

"From Edie. In your honor." When she reached the bedroom, Mary Ellen turned and slipped into his arms. "Now, let's start by compromising, my beloved. I'll take off your clothes if you take off mine," she suggested, her voice husky with desire and love.

And he did.

This month's
irresistible novels from

DREAMS Rita Clay Estrada

Greg Torrance was perfect—gorgeous, successful and offering
her a job! Before she knew it, Mary Ellen Gallagher was
thoroughly seduced. But then she began to suspect Greg's heart
belonged to someone else. Was he too good to be true?

SEDUCING SULLIVAN Julie Elizabeth Leto

Blaze

Angela Harris had only one obsession—sexy-as-sin Jack
Sullivan. Ever since her school days he'd been on her mind…and
in her fantasies. Now she intended to have him in her bed, too!
She thought one sizzling night with Jack would get him out of
her system—but she hadn't counted on Jack having his own
ideas.

HUNK OF THE MONTH JoAnn Ross

The last thing in the world Lucky O'Neill wanted to do was pose
for the cover of a magazine. He was a *man* not a model! But to
help his sister he'd do almost anything. And now that he had met
the magazine editor, Jude Lancaster, taking off his clothes had
more and more appeal…

MANHUNTING IN MISSISSIPPI Stephanie Bond

Manhunting

Piper Shepherd was looking for a husband and finding one
wasn't easy in her small town. But Piper had a plan! She dug out
her grandmother's manhunting manual and gave herself a
makeover. When gorgeous Ian Bentley came to town, the *new*
Piper Shepherd was ready for him!

Spoil yourself next month
with these four novels from

STRUCK BY SPRING FEVER! by Kate Hoffmann

The Men of Bachelor Creek

Sydney Winthrop wasn't one to back down from a challenge—
even if it meant spending a week in the Alaskan wilderness.
Cold nights, bears, mosquitoes...she thought she was ready for
anything...until she met her guide, Hawk. Hard, lean and
sexy-as-sin, this man was more *dangerous* than everything else
put together!

BLACK VELVET by Carrie Alexander

Blaze

Shy Amalie Dove had caused a sensation writing *very* sexy
stories under the name Madame X. Her true identity, however,
had remained a secret until Thomas Jericho started investigating.
Would he expose her? Maybe...but first he wanted to explore
some of the hidden passions that her writing had revealed...

THE PRINCESS AND THE P.I. by Donna Sterling

Being a billionaire heiress wasn't all it was cracked up to be.
Claire Richmond had had enough of her sheltered life. She
wanted freedom! When Claire did made a break for it, she met
gorgeous, *exciting* Tyce Walker... He seemed to want *her* and
not just her money, but could she trust him?

SINGLE IN THE SADDLE by Vicki Lewis Thompson

Mail Order Men

Daphne Proctor wanted a husband, which was when she saw
Stony Arnett's advert in a magazine. Once they'd met face to
face—and she'd felt the sizzling chemistry between them—
Daphne was sure he was *the one*! But then she discovered that,
though Stony had willingly taken her to his bed, *he* hadn't been
the one advertising for a wife!

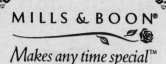

MILLS & BOON®

Makes any time special™

Bestselling themed romances brought back to you by popular demand

Each month By Request brings you three full-length novels in one beautiful volume featuring the best of the best.

So if you missed a favourite Romance the first time around, here is your chance to relive the magic from some of our most popular authors.

Look out for
Sole Paternity **in March 1999**
featuring Miranda Lee, Robyn Donald
and Sandra Marton

MILLS & BOON®

Nearly
Weds!

From your favourite romance authors:

Betty Neels
Making Sure of Sarah

Carole Mortimer
The Man She'll Marry

Penny Jordan
They're Wed Again!

Enjoy an eventful trip to the altar with
three new wedding stories—when
nearly weds become *newly weds!*

Available from 19th March 1999

FREE

2 BOOKS
AND A SURPRISE GIFT!

We would like to take this opportunity to thank you for reading this Mills & Boon® book by offering you the chance to take TWO more specially selected titles from the Temptation® series absolutely FREE! We're also making this offer to introduce you to the benefits of the Reader Service™ —

- ★ FREE home delivery
- ★ FREE monthly Newsletter
- ★ FREE gifts and competitions
- ★ Exclusive Reader Service discounts
- ★ Books available before they're in the shops

Accepting these FREE books and gift places you under no obligation to buy; you may cancel at any time, even after receiving your free shipment. Simply complete your details below and return the entire page to the address below. *You don't even need a stamp!*

YES! Please send me 2 free Temptation books and a surprise gift. I understand that unless you hear from me, I will receive 4 superb new titles every month for just £2.40 each, postage and packing free. I am under no obligation to purchase any books and may cancel my subscription at any time. The free books and gift will be mine to keep in any case.

T9EC

Ms/Mrs/Miss/Mr ....Initials ....
BLOCK CAPITALS PLEASE
Surname...
Address...
....
....Postcode ....

Send this whole page to:
THE READER SERVICE, FREEPOST CN81, CROYDON, CR9 3WZ
(Eire readers please send coupon to: P.O. Box 4546, DUBLIN 24.)

MILLS & BOON®

A man for mum!

Mills & Boon® makes Mother's Day
special by bringing you three new
full-length novels by three of our
most popular Mills & Boon authors:

Penny Jordan

Leigh Michaels

Vicki Lewis Thompson

On Sale 22nd January 1999